ALL IS FAIR IN FOOD AND WAR

Samantha Baca

Contents

One

Kat

"I need a rack of lamb, a sirloin medium, and steamed mussels," I called out, sliding the ticket to the side as the kitchen staff buzzed around me. It was a bustling Friday night which meant that Ambrosia would have a line out the door with people trying to get a seat, even though we were booked three months out with reservations.

I focused on the tray that was ready to go out, making sure everything was perfect. As executive chef, it was my job to ensure that every dish that went out was exactly as it had been ordered and that our signature style was reflected in the presentation. We weren't Seattle's premier and most sought-after restaurant for nothing!

"Looks wonderful, thank you, Lauren." I smiled at the server as she lifted the tray and carried it out.

A few more orders came through, and I was pleased that almost everything was correct, minus a few minor details. However, I tried to be gentle as I coached our newest chef, Javier, on what he had missed. I knew that most kitchens of our status would feel somewhat like stepping into Hell's Kitchen, but I prided myself on treating everyone with respect. You didn't become a world-famous chef by belittling others.

Once the orders were corrected, I gave Javier a pat on the back and went about checking the rest.

"Hey, do you think I could borrow a cup of sugar?"

My head turned toward the velvety smooth voice. The question hadn't been asked of me, and now I knew why.

"Why don't you make sure you have the supplies you need before you open?" I asked, stepping beside Jamie, who was blushing as Miles gave her the smile that usually got him whatever he wanted.

He leaned forward, resting against the counter that separated us.

"Hey, Kat, you're looking good tonight." He gave me a cheeky smile and raised his brows.

I tilted my head and sighed.

"Really? You've sunken as low as sweet talking me for a cup of sugar?"

"Would you like me to earn it some other way? Because I'm totally open to suggestions."

He rubbed his plump lips together, and I heard a soft whimper escape from Jamie. I subtly nudged her with my elbow, and she jerked to attention and then rushed off. She was the sous-chef which meant that she needed to be focused on what was happening in the kitchen and not on the flirty buffoon standing in front of me.

"If you paid attention to your inventory, you wouldn't need to constantly come by asking us for stuff," I said sharply, trying not to let his green eyes lock onto mine.

"I thought I had plenty, but then I launched this new caramel cheesecake dessert tonight, and it's been more popular than I'd imagined. I ran short." He shrugged as if it was an everyday thing to run out of ingredients when you were working in food service. But I guess for him, it was.

"Fine," I sighed. "But this is the last time, and I mean it. If you're going to run a food truck, then you need to learn how to manage it."

"Yes, ma'am," he replied before biting his lip.

I ignored the way my stomach flip-flopped and grabbed two cups of sugar from the kitchen.

"I assume this is all that you need tonight?" I asked. "I can't afford to have my staff constantly distracted, so if you need something else, let's just get it over with now."

He leaned in close as he took the sugar. His mouth hovered just above my ear, sending a shiver through me as the warmth of his breath trailed down it.

"I'll take a date if you're handing them out."

"In your dreams." I pulled back and arched an eyebrow.

"Can't blame me for trying," he laughed and then stepped back. He turned to leave, then stopped and spun around to face me. "Just so you know, you're always in my dreams," he announced loud enough for the entire kitchen to hear. "Even the wet ones."

My face flamed with embarrassment as he tossed a wink at me and left.

I could hear the murmured voices as the kitchen buzzed around me. I turned and caught everyone's attention as they stopped what they were doing and froze.

"Alright, the fun is over. We have work to do. Get those plates over to the expo now. We're about to be in the weeds here. Let's go!"

I walked through the kitchen, checking the different stations and making sure that everything was on track. Miles had stirred everything up and created a vibe in here that left everyone buzzing with excitement—even me—though I hated to admit it. If we wanted a successful night, I needed to get everyone refocused.

"Chef, the guest at table nineteen sent their sirloin back," Emily said as she showed me the returned plate. I peeked at the cut mark in the steak and noticed it was rare.

I grabbed the ticket from the rail and checked it.

"Javier, the sirloin for table nineteen was supposed to be well done, and this was sent out rare. We need to flash it on the fly." I took the plate from Emily and passed it back to Javier.

"Sorry, Chef."

I nodded and continued checking trays as they were brought to me. Soon, I felt back in the groove and forgot about the frenzy Miles Sexton had caused with his flirty banter. I'd known him ever since he parked his obnoxiously big food truck right outside two months ago and never moved.

Once it started to slow down, Jamie joined me at the front of the kitchen and watched the staff as they bustled about, finishing up the last few orders of the night.

"So, are you going to give in and let Miles take you out on a date?" she asked, looking up at me.

I frowned and shook my head.

"Why not? He's soooo hot."

"Then you date him."

"Helllooo, I'm married." She held her hand up and wiggled her fingers in front of me, showing me the simple gold band she wore to work.

"Well then, consider yourself lucky. Miles is a total player and is just looking to get laid."

"Sorry for being blunt, but I wouldn't say no to that," she laughed and shrugged before pushing off the counter to go talk with the server before they delivered their order.

I knew Miles' kind and could recognize what he wanted a mile away because I had been engaged to a guy just like him. That's why I made it my mission to avoid him every chance I got.

Two
Miles

"Man, those cheesecake bars really sold out tonight," Anthony said, leaning against the counter. He'd been my best friend since we were in college and helped me start up the Miles High Food Club, a food truck that served a random assortment of sandwiches and fried foods, depending on my mood.

"I didn't expect them to be so popular."

"I think after the first girl said that they tasted better than sex, that was all the advertising we needed. You know how good word of mouth works." He chuckled and folded his arms over his broad chest.

"I told you to take one to Kat; you probably would've scored that date you've been after."

I smiled a crooked grin, knowing that he was right.

I looked over at the shelf behind us with five full bags of sugar and then at the container she'd given me when I'd gone over to ask for some. It was stupid, but I felt the need to get her attention any way that I could.

There was something about her that really got under my skin. Anthony was convinced that it was because she was the only girl who had ever rejected me when I'd asked them out, but I knew it was something deeper than that. Maybe it was her fiery attitude every time I talked to her, or maybe it was because I could tell she wasn't interested in me because of my looks like most girls seemed to be. I was thirty years old and had long outgrown the superficial aspect of dating. I wanted someone I could grow old with and get to know without worrying about them hiding the second they washed their makeup off.

"Did you want to go get a beer," Anthony asked. "Or are we waiting for Kat to leave so you can watch her and pretend that you're not secretly obsessed with her?"

"I'm not obsessed with her," I said over my shoulder as I wiped down the counter and tossed the rag into the pile of laundry that I needed to do tonight.

But he was right. I was delaying and taking longer to shut down tonight, because I was waiting to see her.

"You're such a terrible liar."

I was about to throw some sarcastic comment back at him, but the door to Ambrosia opened, and I saw Kat walk out with Jamie. They were laughing at something, and I could see the way Kat's brown eyes sparkled. Her dark curly hair was pulled down, barely brushing against her shoulders as she walked.

I rarely got to see her outside of work, which meant that I appreciated every chance I had of seeing her wearing something other than the pressed white button-down shirt, black dress slacks, and apron that hid her body. If I had to guess, the girls were going out tonight, given that she was wearing a low-cut black dress that wrapped tightly around her curvy body and hit mid-thigh.

I watched which direction they were headed and smiled when I saw them pull the door open to Seven Sins to slip inside. The music floated out of the bar.

"Yeah, a beer sounds great," I said casually.

"Let me guess, we're going to Seven Sins?"

I winked at my best friend, who stood there shaking his head at how pathetic I was. One way or another, I was going to get Kat Elliott to notice me.

Three
Kat

"How about that booth in the corner?" I asked Jamie, pointing to it in case she couldn't hear me over the music that was blaring around us. When she'd asked me to go out for a drink, I'd been inclined to say no. I changed my mind when I saw the disappointed look on her face, and heard that her husband had to work late tonight.

Seven Sins was a popular bar, but it wasn't my usual scene. I'd much prefer staying at home to read a book and enjoy a glass of wine than to have to yell over the music and fight off frat guys who wanted to gyrate on the dance floor.

She nodded, and I took that as my cue to go grab it before someone else snatched it up. It was busy but not too crowded yet. Most of the people were either lined up at the bar for shots to get the weekend started, or they were already on the dance floor.

I shimmied my way through the crowd, making sure not to let my hands hang low so I didn't accidentally grope anyone in the process of getting to safety. *Safety, I snorted. Why did being twenty-eight feel so similar to being in my eighties?*

I was almost to the booth when I felt someone grab my elbow and stop me.

"Dance with me, baby," a much too young guy said, giving me a lopsided grin and trying to pull me back to the dance floor.

"No thanks, I'm allergic to dancing." I gave him a fake

smile and escaped his grasp as he stood there trying to figure out what I'd said. It didn't matter whether it made sense or not; I'd gotten away, and that was the goal.

I jumped into the booth and took the side against the wall to people-watch. It was the equivalent of watching reality TV as drunken shenanigans were sure to happen tonight.

A few minutes later, Jamie slid into the other side of the booth and slid a manhattan my way.

"Thanks," I said, taking a sip.

"No problem." She lifted the bottle of beer to her lips and took a swig.

"It's busy already," she said, turning sideways to people watch with me.

"I'm surprised. I thought more people would be heading out of town for spring break."

"Yeah, but a lot of them don't have the money to. With gas prices increasing and flights being outrageously high, I can't imagine that many people will be traveling anytime soon."

"True." I took another drink, knowing that she was right.

While the economy, in general, seemed to be struggling, I was thankful that Ambrosia hadn't been impacted by it. We had steady increases in reservations requests and were constantly featured on different social media outlets. One of the biggest reasons for our success was that Ambrosia was owned and operated by an incredible woman who cared about others and not making a fortune off of them. Clarissa had been the talk of Seattle and recently had recruiters from other states reaching out to her.

We finished our first round of drinks, and then I headed to the bar for a second. We could have waited for the cocktail waitress to make her way to us, but it looked like she was the only one on the floor tonight and had two six tops waiting on her, plus an eight top in the corner. Not wanting to add to her stress tonight, we'd decided we'd take care of getting our own drinks.

I stood to the side, waiting for the bartender to come back. He was busy at the other end of the bar, flirting with a group of girls wearing bride-themed sashes. I rolled my eyes and looked around to see where the other bartender had gone.

The bar continued to fill up, and the thick mass of bodies on the dance floor increased the temperature in the place. I brushed my hair away from my face, regretting that I'd let Jamie talk me into wearing it down tonight. It was short but thick and suddenly felt like it weighed a hundred pounds.

While I waited, I pulled the hair tie off of my wrist and began piling my hair on top of my head before securing it. As I lowered my arm, I felt somebody beside me and accidentally elbowed them.

"I'm so sorry," I apologized, turning to see Miles beside me.

My face quickly morphed from apologetic to irritated in seconds.

"What are you doing here?" I asked grumpily as he slid in closer, invading my space. His back was facing the other people in line at the bar as he faced me. I could feel the heat from his body radiating off of him, making me hotter than I already was.

"I came with my friend to have a drink."

A cocky smile pulled at the corners of his lips.

"You sure you're not following me?"

Even though I hadn't looked in his direction when we'd left earlier, I'd felt his eyes on me and knew that he was watching us.

"Do you want me to follow you?"

"No."

"Are you sure? We could turn it into a game. I can be the lost, lonely puppy looking for my owner…."

I looked up and locked eyes with him.

"Are you saying you want me to own you?"

He clicked his tongue against the roof of his mouth as he thought about his answer.

"I wouldn't be opposed to it."

My cheeks flushed with heat, just in time for the bartender to show up and ask what we wanted.

"Manhattan and a Corona, please." I fidgeted with the edge of the bar, feeling overly anxious being this close to Miles.

"For you?" the bartender asked Miles, assuming we were together.

"Oh no, his is separate. We're not together," I clarified.

"We're not. But we could be," he added with a wink. "Please put her drinks on my tab. I'll take two bourbons, neat." He pulled his wallet out and laid his credit card in front of us.

"You're not buying my drinks," I insisted in a hushed tone as the bartender left to make our drinks.

"Come on, Kat. Why are you so mean to me? Can't I just buy you a drink?"

"No."

"Why not?"

"Because then you'll think I owe you something, and I don't."

He pulled back as if my words had inflicted pain.

"Why would I think you owe me something? It's a drink, Kat. Not a kidney."

"Trust me, I know how guys operate. You buy my drinks, and that automatically translates to you expecting a blow job—at minimum."

He shook his head in disbelief and leaned his arm on the counter.

"Is that the kind of guys you've met? Because you might need to try different places to meet men. Real men. Not these frat kids walking around, thinking with their cocks."

I pulled my shoulders back and looked around for the bartender. Why was this taking so long?

"I don't go out to look for men," I replied quickly. "But yes, the ones I've met have expected something in return. Everyone does, Miles. Even you."

His hand gently reached out and brushed against my side before settling on my hip. He leaned in close, and the smell of his cologne wafted up around us.

"Trust me, if I buy you a drink, I don't expect a damn thing in return. If I buy you a meal, I don't expect anything other than that you'll enjoy it. And if I were ever given a chance to be with you, the only thing that I would want is for you to experience all of the pleasure I could give you—without expecting anything in return."

My body froze under his touch, my words lodged in my throat.

"Find yourself someone who wants to give you everything, Kat, and you'd be surprised by how good it can feel."

He pulled back and dropped his hand as the bartender returned with our drinks. I tried to pull my jaw back up from the floor as I carried our drinks back to our booth with Miles right behind me.

I didn't get a chance to give Jamie a heads-up that he was there before he slipped into the booth beside me. A few minutes later, his friend Anthony joined us, and I found myself glaring at her as she grinned a shit-eating smile as she watched Miles scoot closer to me.

My body was tense and rigid as my brain argued with it about all of the reasons why we shouldn't let our guard down and let him in, no matter how good it felt when he touched me a few minutes ago. He was just like Nick, and I needed to remember that.

<u>Four</u>
Miles

The bass thumped against the walls, making it hard to hear what Jamie was saying. Between the four of us, she was the only one holding the conversation, and the majority of it was with Anthony. It turned out they both grew up in small towns close to each other in Illinois, something neither Kat, nor I, had any clue about.

I wanted to ask Kat if she wanted to dance, but her body was wound tighter than a clock as she stuffed herself as far into the booth as possible, so she didn't have to touch me. This wasn't how most of my dates went. I reminded myself that this wasn't a date and Kat wasn't anything like the women I'd dated since I'd moved to Seattle a few months ago.

I had grown up in southern California and stayed there until my grandfather passed away. My grandma needed help but refused to ask. I had always been close to my grandparents and couldn't stand the thought of my grandma living in Seattle by herself. So, I'd given up everything I had in California and moved here without giving it a second thought. I haven't regretted it once.

"Is there anything I can get you?" the waitress asked as she stopped by our table. The bar was almost to capacity, with bodies smushed together on the dance floor and every table occupied.

"Would you like another?" I asked Kat, leaning in so she could hear me.

Her eyes widened as if she thought I might kiss her, and

I found myself smiling at the thought. Did I make her nervous? All this time, I just thought she hated me but didn't know why.

"Sure," she said softly, forcing me to read her lips to know what she'd said.

I ordered another round for Kat and me, leaving Jamie and Anthony to take care of their own. After the waitress left, I leaned into Kat and attempted to talk to her again.

"So, what will it take for me to get you to take me up on that date offer?" I asked, leaving enough space between us to avoid crowding her or making her feel uncomfortable.

She turned and studied my face, the dimly lit room making her eyes look even darker with the smokey makeup she was wearing.

"Why do you want to take me out so badly?"

"Why wouldn't I?"

"You don't even know me."

"That's usually the point of taking someone out. You hang out, have dinner, or a few drinks. Talk. Get to know each other."

Her eyes narrowed.

"You haven't had a lot of good dates, have you?"

"That's none of your business."

She turned away, breaking eye contact with me.

"Look, I can tell that you don't trust me, and I don't blame you."

That got her attention as her head turned back to me.

"You shouldn't trust someone that you don't know. All I'm asking for is the chance to get to know each other."

"I still don't get why you want this so badly."

"You interest me."

"Why?"

"I don't know," I laughed, sinking against the booth as my body relaxed. "I haven't figured that out, but there's something about you that's different than anyone I've ever met. It makes me curious and want to get to know you."

"I'm not that interesting." She jutted her chin out and turned her hair again.

The waitress returned with our drinks, shutting down any witty response I might've come up with to counter her.

We drank our drinks, sitting there in awkward silence as Jamie and Anthony finished up their conversation. Jamie checked her phone and then frowned.

"Sorry, Jim is getting off work, so I gotta go. Do you want me to drive you home?" She looked at Kat and the brand new drink sitting in front of her.

"Yeah," Kat hesitated. "Or I can just catch a cab."

"I don't want you taking a cab this late, I can let Jim know I'll be a few minutes late if you want to finish your drink."

"It'll take more than a few minutes unless you want me wasted in your car for the ride home. It's not a big deal, really. I used to take cabs all the time; it's fine."

"I can take you home," I offered, speaking loudly so they could both hear me. I glanced at Jamie, noticing the smug smile on her face before I turned to Kat. "I don't mind."

"No, it's fine, really."

"I agree with Jamie, I don't think it's safe for you to take a cab home by yourself. Especially when you've been drinking. I'm more than happy to take you."

She seemed frustrated, looking between us, then down at her drink.

"I haven't had that much to drink. If I don't finish this one, then I've only had two. I'm barely buzzed and can punch someone in the throat if needed."

I arched a brow and felt Jamie's eyes on me.

"Okay, well, I'm going to get going. I'll check on you later," she said, pointing a finger at Kat.

"Alright, tell Jim hi."

I gave her a slight wave as Anthony stood up and offered to walk her to her car. I knew that it was his way of calling it a night as well so he could get home to his girlfriend when she got out of work.

"Looks like it's just us," I said, noting the irritation still etched on her face. "Why don't we finish these, then go dance off some of the alcohol?"

I wasn't anywhere near buzzed and had nursed the first drink for over an hour before the waitress brought this one. I had no plans of throwing it back, but when I saw Kat chug hers, I did the same.

She nodded for me to get up, so I chuckled and slid out of the booth, stepping to the side and extending my hand to help her up. Holding her chin high, she climbed out and ignored the hand I'd offered her.

We made our way to the dance floor, squeezing in between people as they bounced around to the upbeat song that was currently playing. It wasn't my type of music, but at least it was easy to move to.

Kat closed her eyes as she moved her body, letting the rhythm guide her. I wanted to reach out and touch her but trusted what she'd said a few minutes ago about punching someone in the throat tonight, and I didn't want to be the person on the receiving end of that threat.

But then, out of nowhere, a burly guy knocked into me, sending me right in her direction. I placed my hands around her waist to keep from tackling her as I stepped to the side to catch my balance.

Her eyes opened, studying me with curiosity as my hands stayed glued to her waist. She turned around, pressed her back to my chest, and clasped her hands over mine. I expected her to push me away, but instead, she began moving with the beat, swaying her hips and brushing her ass against my groin.

I closed my eyes and groaned at the friction, fighting the erection that wanted to make a special guest appearance. Now wasn't the time to act like a fifteen-year-old boy who'd just seen boobs for the first time. I needed to prove to Kat that I wasn't like the other guys she'd dated and that I wasn't just looking for a hookup.

With my eyes closed, I pictured my grandma standing at the stove, making spaghetti, and allowed the memories to wash away the erotic thoughts I'd had of Kat just seconds before.

My hands slid down her waist and held onto her hips as I moved with her. It felt like no one else was around us as we danced, our bodies in sync with each other, speaking a secret language that even I couldn't understand.

"You're so beautiful," I growled into her ear, feeling her body react to my words.

I wanted to keep touching her and dancing but knew that sooner than later, my erection was going to make a comeback. It was impossible for it not to, given how she was caressing my dick with every move she made.

"Why don't we head over to my food truck, and I'll fix us some food, then take you home?"

She spun around, her brown eyes slightly hooded. Satisfaction blossomed in my chest, knowing she'd been just as affected by this as I had.

"I'm not asking for anything in return, Kat. Just let me feed you and make sure you get home, okay? Nothing more than that."

She nodded and took a deep breath.

I held her hand as I led us through the packed bar and out to the sidewalk as a breeze whipped past us. It was a short walk to the truck, which was helpful given the heels she was wearing.

She shivered slightly and rubbed her hands up and down her arms while I unlocked the back and helped her inside. I pulled the door closed and offered her to take a seat.

"Is there anything you feel like?" I asked, not sure what she wanted.

"I'm good with whatever, you don't even have to cook for me."

"I know I don't have to. I want to. What would you like?"

"Surprise me."

I picked up on the sassiness in her tone, knowing that she was challenging me to impress her. Little did she know, I had a lot of skills both in and out of the kitchen.

I glanced at my phone, realizing it was almost one in the morning. She'd had a decent amount to drink and was being nice to me, which made me think she might've been more than buzzed.

Deciding on something quick and easy, I fired up the grill and cooked a few hotdogs and some onion rings. I looked over my shoulder as I heard a noise come out of her mouth that sounded vaguely like a moan.

"Eat this; it'll help you avoid a hangover tomorrow." I handed her a plate and then sat down beside her and started eating mine.

"I'm not drunk," she insisted, followed by a hiccup. She covered her mouth and giggled while I enjoyed seeing her vulnerable for once.

"Alright, Wonder Woman. Just eat your damn hotdog and stop fighting with me."

"I like fighting with you." She took a bite, then closed her eyes and groaned. "Your wiener is so delicious. I could eat this all day."

I swallowed hard, nearly choking on my bite. Okay, she was definitely drunk, and now I couldn't think about anything other than Kat eating my wiener.

Five
Kat

"Mmmm, right there," I moaned, my eyes pinched closed as I felt his tongue slide between my folds.

He gripped my thighs tighter, spreading me open as he kissed and nipped at my already sensitive clit. It was pure torture and heaven at the same time. His fingers slid inside and curled up, hitting my g-spot with conviction.

"Oh, God." I panted and bucked off of the bed, pressing my thighs closed. It was too much, and I was on sensation overload.

"I don't think so," he growled, forcing my legs open as he wedged his way even deeper. "I want to hear you scream, Kat. I want my name on your lips as your orgasm rips through you. I want to know that this pussy is mine and that the pleasure you get is what I give you. Now be a good girl and spread your legs for me."

I whimpered and bit down on my hand as his tongue flicked rapidly against my clit and his fingers moved quickly inside of me.

"Yes," I cried, allowing my body to convulse around him as he sucked harder and drew the orgasm out of me. I dug my nails into the sheets, gripping them as I struggled to hold on.

Once it was over, I looked down to see Miles wiping his mouth and a look of pure satisfaction on his face.

My breathing was erratic as I tried to sit up. I wanted more—no, I needed more.

"Come here," I said, curling my finger into a come hither motion.

He slowly crawled up the bed after stripping off his pants and boxer briefs. His cock was thick and ready, with a drop of cum glistening on the tip. I licked my lips, desperate to taste it.

"I want you to fuck me," I whispered, reaching for him.

Then suddenly, he was gone, and my eyes fluttered open. I sat up and looked around the room, feeling my heart pounding inside my chest, disappointed that it had been a dream.

I plopped back down on the mattress and groaned. I'd had a sex dream about a guy I wanted nothing to do with, and it just happened to be the best damn dream ever. Not only that, I'd actually had an orgasm in my sleep, which never happened.

I climbed out of bed feeling frustrated and turned on the shower. I was going to need a cold one to wash away the thoughts of that stupid dream before I had to see Miles tonight. It was Saturday which meant that we would be busy, and he would have his food truck set up again.

I'd asked Clarissa why she allowed him to park in front of Ambrosia when he first started and she simply shrugged and said that it didn't hurt having him there. It wasn't like there was much she could do anyway, given that he was parked by the sidewalk where the other food trucks had lined up. His just happened to be right in front of her restaurant, whereas the others were in front of other businesses and not direct competition.

But she was right; he wasn't our competition, given that we didn't serve the same type of food. He focused on sandwiches and fried foods, while we prided ourselves on offering more elegant dishes. We were completely different.

I finished my shower and then ran a few errands before heading into Ambrosia. We didn't open until four and had our daily staff meeting to discuss the special and menu changes at three. I liked to go in early so I could try out new dish ideas and run them by Clarissa when it wasn't busy, and she could focus.

As I headed toward the restaurant, I found myself looking to see if Miles was already there. It didn't surprise me that he got there early, but I couldn't help but wonder why he didn't spend some of that time stocking up on the supplies he needed so he didn't have to come borrow stuff from Ambrosia all the time. Just like clockwork, I spotted his truck sitting out front in the same spot it always was.

My stomach fluttered as I remembered last night at the bar and then him taking me to his truck and cooking food for me. It hadn't been anything fancy, but it was delicious, to say the least. I'd been thankful this morning when I woke up without the slight threat of a hangover. Granted, I didn't drink that much, but I was more of a lightweight, and it didn't take much.

I was so distracted looking for him inside the truck that I hadn't been paying attention and almost walked into a light pole. I noticed it at the last second and jumped to the side, my heart racing in response.

Embarrassed, I pulled my jacket tighter around me and rushed into Ambrosia, hoping no one had seen me.

"You're here early," Clarissa said, looking up at the clock on the wall across from her. She had the reservation list for tonight in her hand as she stood at the hostess station.

"It's not that early. Barely after one-thirty."

"You don't usually come in until two."

"Yeah, but I wanted to try something new and didn't want to rush."

"Please tell me that it's a dessert," she pleaded with her hands together in front of her. "After Miles's caramel cheesecake bars last night, people have been talking nonstop about them. I know he's not our competition, but I would love to have a new dessert to get people's attention."

I pulled my mouth to the side and slid out of my jacket. I

had planned on trying a new vegetarian dish, but I couldn't say no if Clarissa really wanted a new dessert.

"I can talk to Pam when she gets here," I offered, knowing that it would be better to bounce ideas off our pastry chef. She did desserts like no one I knew, and I felt like I might disappoint Clarissa on my own.

"I would love to see what *you* come up with." Her tone was gentle, but there was a challenge in her eyes.

I took a deep breath and slowly let it out, squaring my shoulders in response.

"I'll see what I can do."

"Excellent."

As I was walking to the back, I heard the bell ding on the front door and turned to see who it was.

"Hey, I wanted to bring this back," Miles said before lifting his head to see me standing in the doorway. "Oh, hey. How are you feeling?"

"I'm fine." I stood frozen in place as Clarissa curiously looked between us.

"Why wouldn't she be fine? What's wrong?"

"Nothing," I replied sharply. "I'm fine."

"Sorry, I was just checking," Miles said and shoved his hands in his pockets as Clarissa held the stack of bowls he'd returned from the things he borrowed last week.

"Okay, something is going on, and I want to know what it is. One of you spill it, now." She pointed a finger between us and waited.

"I went to Seven Sins with Jamie last night. Miles was there. We had a few drinks, and then he made food for us before driving me home. Nothing happened."

"I just wanted to make sure you were feeling okay, that's all."

"Well, that was nice of you," Clarissa said with a cheeky grin. "What did you make her?"

"A hotdog and onion rings," I blurted out, feeling more defensive than I should. "Nothing spectacular."

I noticed the look that flashed across his face when I said it and instantly felt like the world's biggest bitch. Why did I have this reaction to him every time he was around? I was guarded and felt the need to protect myself, though he'd never given me a reason to.

"Sorry," I apologized. "The food was good; I didn't mean to sound so insulting."

He rocked back on his heels and gave me a smug smile.

"Don't worry about it. You'd know if I were trying to impress you with my cooking."

I took a few steps toward him, ignoring the stars dancing in Clarissa's eyes as she watched us.

"What's that supposed to mean?"

"It means that last night was a no-effort attempt to get food in you so you didn't wake up with a hangover. *If* I wanted to, I could out cook you any day."

"Is that so?" I placed my hand on my hip and stared at him as he closed the space between us.

Our chests were almost touching as he towered slightly over me. The scent of his cologne was almost intoxicating, but not nearly as much as the green eyes that locked onto mine.

"I guarantee you've never had anything as good as my food."

"I highly doubt that."

"Wanna bet?"

"That you can cook food that I'll like? No, not really."

"Is this a power struggle? Because I gotta admit, I might be into it." He wiggled his brows and leaned closer to whisper something that only I could hear. "I'm not afraid to let a woman take control, if you know what I mean."

I hated the gasp that escaped my lips, but not as much as I hated the way my thighs were clenched together, and heat was spreading through me as I thought about him in my dream last night.

"What's the matter, cat got your tongue?" he prodded, licking his lips before pulling the bottom one between his teeth.

I tried to suck in a deep breath so I could get the oxygen that I needed to clear my brain, but unfortunately, it was filled with his scent, which only made me feel even more intoxicated.

"I'm not going to play this game with you," I bit out, taking a step back on wobbly legs.

"Why not? Afraid you'll lose?"

"Lose what? We didn't bet anything."

"Alright," he said casually, pushing his sleeves up to his elbows and revealing tattoos I didn't know he had. "How about a friendly cook-off to see who the better chef is?"

"That's not a fair competition, and you know it." I folded my arms over my chest protectively.

"Then what are you so worried about?" He cocked his head to the side and held my gaze.

"Fine," I breathed. "What do you have in mind?"

He rubbed his hands together excitedly and looked from Clarissa to me.

"We have a three-course competition to see who the better cook is. If I win, you go on a date with me."

"And when I win?"

"You can take me on a date," he teased, wiggling his eyebrows.

"Funny."

"Okay, fine, if you win, then I'll never ask you out again. I'll leave you alone and won't bother you."

I felt Clarissa's eyes on me as they waited for my answer.

"Fine, you have yourself a cook-off." I reached out and shook the hand he extended to me.

"I can't believe this," Clarissa said excitedly. "If you guys are okay with it, I can organize everything here, and we'll make an event out of it?"

"That'd be great," Miles said, keeping his eyes on me and not bothering to look at her as he spoke.

"You're going down, Miles," I replied sarcastically, not realizing the weight of my words until I noticed how his eyes darkened and trailed down between my thighs.

"I really hope so." He licked his lips again, and I felt my face flush.

Without saying another word, I turned on my heel and headed to the kitchen, leaving the two of them to discuss the details of this absurd competition.

<u>Six</u>
Miles

My body was buzzing with excitement after I left Ambrosia. I knew Kat doubted my ability to cook anything besides a basic sandwich, and I couldn't wait to prove her wrong.

I'd spent the next few hours hurrying to prep as much as I could before our rush tonight. Anthony was supposed to be there by five but texted to let me know he was running late. I quickly replied to him and then started working the line of customers already waiting when I opened.

Tonight's menu was Latin inspired after I had the sudden urge to mix things up. I had an assortment of tacos listed on the board, along with the cheesecake bars from last night. While I would have preferred to do a dessert that went with the theme, I didn't have enough time to prepare it.

By the time Anthony had shown up, I had a line wrapped around the corner and was low on oil to fry the taco shells. I had texted him and asked if he could grab some on his way, but he didn't get the message until he got there.

He was quicker at taking orders while I cooked, so I left him to tend to the line while I darted out of the back of the truck and rushed into Ambrosia. For once, I was actually in need of the item I was there to ask for.

The hostess nodded at me as I headed back to the kitchen. It happened so often now that I was almost an honorary employee, and no one batted an eye at my presence other than Kat.

I slipped between the doors as a waiter carried a tray past, pulling my body to the side so I didn't bump it. I looked around the busy room, noticing everyone was focused and shouting orders at each other.

Then I found Kat and Jamie standing by the expo station, waiting for plates to come their way. I was about to clear my throat to let them know I was standing behind them when I heard Kat whispering to Jamie.

"It was so intense, and now I can't look at him without thinking about the damn dream."

"You're so lucky," Jamie whined. "I can't remember the last time I had an orgasm in my sleep."

"You don't get it, this is a real problem," Kat hissed.

"Why?"

"Because I dreamt about Miles eating me out!"

"Yeah, and you said that in your dream, it felt amazing. Better than anything you'd ever felt before. I don't see what the problem is."

"It was too real; it was like I could feel the way his tongue—"

"Ahem," I cleared my throat, knowing that I needed to make my presence known before someone in the kitchen said something, and it embarrassed Kat even more than she was going to be, knowing that I'd just overheard her talking to Jamie.

She spun around, her hand clutching her chest as her eyes widened in horror.

"I'm so sorry to interrupt, but do you guys, by chance, have some oil I can borrow? I asked Anthony to stop and get some on his way in, but he didn't get my text in time. We're busier than I'd anticipated and are almost out."

Kat's face was beet red, making her look even more adorable.

"Sure," Jamie said, pushing away from the counter to grab some.

"How much of that did you hear?" Kat asked with her eyes closed and her hand covering her face.

"Only as much as you wanted me to hear."

I wasn't going to lie and pretend I hadn't heard them. That was by far the hottest thing I'd ever heard a woman say, and my dick agreed as it pressed against the zipper of my jeans. I subtly reached down and tried to adjust myself.

"None?"

I shrugged and bit back a laugh.

"Okay, none it is."

She peeked at me through her fingers, then sighed.

"You heard all of it, didn't you?" she muttered.

"I'm not sure what I missed before you got to the good part. Or maybe I was at the good part? It sounded like I was definitely the one getting to the good part, though I wouldn't mind more details about what I was doing."

I looked up as Jamie headed our way.

"You're not going to get them, and as far as I'm concerned, this conversation never happened."

"That's too bad," I sighed, taking the jar from Jamie. "I've been known to make women's dreams come true in bed." I winked, thanked Jamie for the oil, and then rushed back to the truck.

By seven, the line had started to die down as most of the foot traffic was customers heading into Ambrosia for dinner. I'd heard a few leave, commenting on the new salted caramel molten lava cake that Chef Elliott had prepared tonight, and couldn't help but smile at the idea of Kat exploding under my touch the way her cake had done for their customers. While I'd loved that people had called our cheesecake bars orgasmic, people were even more impressed by the cake, and I had a feeling I would get to try it soon. But then again, Kat might surprise me and make a different dessert in the cook-off.

While I didn't know her as well as I wanted to, I knew she preferred to cook more complex meals and didn't care much for desserts. They had an amazing pastry chef that was usually the talk of the town until tonight.

"So, how did last night go?" Anthony asked, taking a sip of water as he sat down on the crates behind us. For once, there was no one in line, so we had a quick break.

"It was fine. We finished our drink, danced a little, and then I brought her back here to make some food for her so she wasn't hung over today."

"What did you make?"

"Hotdogs and onion rings. I was tired, and it was easy."

"How'd she like your *wiener*?"

I rolled my eyes and tried to keep from grinning at his childish joke. I wanted to tell him about the dream conversation I'd overheard but didn't want to embarrass her. It wasn't like she'd told it to me; I'd eavesdropped accidentally. She had been confiding in her friend, and it wasn't my place to tell anyone her business.

"She enjoyed the food."

"Mmhmm," he pulled his lips into a thin line and waited for me to say more.

"Nothing else happened. I took her home, made sure she got in okay, then left."

"So what happened with the oil shortage tonight? Were you

using it to work off some frustration before I got here?"

I shook my head and picked up my water bottle.

"You're disgusting. First of all, I wouldn't use cooking oil. Second, I wouldn't do that here. And third, I'm not fifteen anymore. I don't just jack off 24/7."

"I'm just saying, you've been hard up for her since you first laid eyes on her. I wouldn't blame you if you needed to work off some of that pent-up tension."

A couple of girls walked up and looked at the menu at the same time my phone rang. I looked down to see my grandma's name on the caller ID and nodded for Anthony to help them. He got up and greeted them with his usual flirty tone while I climbed out the back and walked across the street to take the call.

"Hey grandma, everything okay?" I asked as I answered it.

"Yes, dear, you don't have to worry that I'm dying every time I call."

"I know, I'm sorry. I just don't get calls often from you, so you know…"

"That's because we see each other for Sunday dinner every week, and I know you're busy."

"Fair enough," I laughed. "So, what's up?"

"I have a favor to ask."

I sat down on the empty bench and waited for her to ask.

"Okay."

"You don't even know what I'm going to say."

"It doesn't matter. I would do anything for you; you know that."

"Ah, my sweet boy. That's very nice of you, thank you."

"Alright, so what's this favor that you need?"

"Well, my friend Gennie has a granddaughter that is new to town. She's only been here a few weeks and could use someone to show her around, maybe make a few friends."

I felt a knot form in my stomach. I hated being set up, even by my grandma.

"How old is she?"

"Twenty-three."

"I doubt that she wants a thirty-year-old guy showing her around town. Plus, I'm not the kind of friend she needs. She needs girls her age that she can go out with."

"I know, but she's been depressed, and we're worried about her. She's a nice girl, you'll see. Just a little green and inexperienced in life, but still a nice girl."

"I don't know," I sighed, running my hand through my short hair. "I don't really have the time right now."

"Well, I kinda told her to go by your food truck tonight. She should be there soon."

I looked across the street to see a blonde girl standing off to the side, staring down at her phone. She looked to be around the same age and was by herself.

"Fine, I'll take her somewhere tonight, but that's it. No more *friendship dates*," I warned playfully.

"You can't blame a grandma for trying. Have fun, I love you!" She rushed off the phone and hung up.

"You owe me, grandma," I muttered, then headed across the street to introduce myself.

<u>Seven</u>

Kat

"Table six is finishing their appetizers; fire the steaks," I called out, placing the ticket on the rail. "We've also got two orders dying on the pass, where is Rodrigo?"

After Miles left, things felt more chaotic than usual, and I struggled to compose myself in the midst of the kitchen, feeling like it was falling apart.

Jamie stood across the room from me, checking plates before they were taken out.

"Here, Chef," Rodrigo answered as he brushed past me and grabbed the plates from the pass.

"You're good to go; I've already checked them." I nodded toward the door, telling him to get going.

"We've got a customer complaint from table six," Lauren said as she pushed through the doors into the kitchen. "They asked for sauce on the side."

I pinched the bridge of my nose and inhaled deeply.

"We need a chicken francese, sauce on the side. Do not mess this up," I warned, looking across the room as low voices answered with *yes, Chef.*

I took the dish from Lauren and pushed it off to the side with the collection of dead plates that had come back tonight. Either they weren't cooked right, were served overcooked, or simply didn't meet the guest's expectations. I prided myself on rarely having a dead plate, but tonight we had six of them. Clarissa was not going to be happy.

Finally, we were slowing down, and the last few dishes were being served. I pulled myself up onto the cold steel countertop in the corner and watched as the staff wrapped up. We all stayed behind after closing tonight to discuss what happened with Clarissa.

My body ached in a way that didn't happen often, and I knew it was partly due to drinking last night. I was barely twenty-eight, but sometimes my body was convinced that I was sixty and couldn't handle even a single drink or staying up late without paying for it the next day. Or maybe, I was just so used to a calmer lifestyle that going out and trying to keep up with the twenty-one-year-olds was harder than I thought.

Finally, the doors were closed, the last customers had left, and Clarissa joined us in the kitchen. Following right behind her was Miles.

I frowned and wondered what he was doing there. It wasn't like he'd been in the kitchen and responsible for the handful of orders we'd gotten wrong.

"Alright, everyone, I'm going to make this quick. We were not on our game tonight, and our customers received less than stellar from us. I don't know what was happening back here, but I can tell it wasn't just one person. Whatever it is, it stops tonight. If you cannot return to this kitchen tomorrow with a clear head and focused, then don't bother walking through that door. Ambrosia is an elite restaurant in Seattle, and I have the best of the best applying to work here. Don't make me question whether you deserve to be here."

Everyone apologized and kept their heads lowered in embarrassment, including me.

"Okay, now that that's done, I want to discuss something that will be happening in two weeks." She looked beside her at Miles and smiled.

"We're going to be hosting a special cook-off between two of Seattle's best chefs. Our own, Kat Elliott, will be going up against Miles Sexton in an epic battle that will take place right here, in our own kitchen. I'm in the process of finding a few guest judges, but I would love for all of you to be here for it. We'll do it on Sunday when we're closed, so we don't have to worry about impacting reservations."

Everyone talked excitedly around me as I stood there, trying to feel the same excitement they had. It wasn't that I wasn't eager to prove him wrong and beat him in the kitchen, but I was drained from a long, exhausting day and wanted to go home and throw myself in bed.

"Thanks for inviting me to be here for the discussion, but I've gotta go," Miles said, holding Clarissa's elbow as he leaned in to talk to her. "Let me know if there's anything that you need from me; if not, I'll see you on Monday."

"Thanks, Miles." She squeezed his hand as he smiled at me and squeezed past her.

"Why are you seeing him on Monday?"

"I've offered for him to come work in the kitchen for the next two weeks so he can get used to it before the competition. It wouldn't be fair that you know where everything is, and he doesn't."

"What about the food truck?"

"He'll be here for a few hours before we open, then he'll go do his stuff."

"You mean the hours when I come into work?"

She shrugged as a devious smile spread across her face, and I knew she was trying to play matchmaker again.

"It won't hurt you to figure out how to work together and share a space. Plus, I need to make sure you guys don't catch my kitchen on fire with all of that chemistry radiating between the two of you." She winked and walked off.

I attempted to speak, but no words came out.

Eight

Miles

"Sorry I'm late," I extended my hand to shake hers, but she looked confused, so I pulled it back.

"You're Lucinda, right?"

"Yeah. You're Miles?"

I nodded and shoved my hands into my pockets.

"My grandma didn't tell me you'd be so cute," she noted, her blue eyes shining up at me under the streetlamp.

"Umm, thanks." I didn't want to compliment her and make her think this was a date. I'm sure both of our grandmas insinuated it was, but I wasn't about to continue the misconception.

"So, where did you want to go?" I asked, trying to fill the silence. It was just after ten, but there were plenty of places to go on a Saturday night in Seattle.

"I'm not really into the bar scene," she said slowly, giving me a sexy smile. "We could always go to your place and hang out if you want."

I shoved my hands even deeper into my pockets, avoiding hers as it hung low by her side, ready to touch me the moment she thought I gave her the okay.

"I actually know of a nice café that we can go to. It's pretty mellow and has great pastries."

"Okay," she shrugged, seeming disappointed as she pulled her cell phone out and began typing.

We rounded the corner, and I nearly tripped over a pizza box left on the sidewalk by a man who appeared to be sleeping. I paused for a moment and peered at him, making sure he was okay.

"He's out here *all the time*," she muttered, eyes still glued to her phone.

I stopped and knelt beside him, gently tapping his shoe with my hand. It had holes and looked like it was about to fall apart, as did the other one.

"Mhhmhm," he grumbled a jargon of words, but his eyes fluttered open. He pulled back instinctively, so I leaned back, giving him space so he knew I wasn't a threat.

The man looked between us, a layer of dirt on his face and sadness in his eyes. Then he noticed the pizza box in the middle of the sidewalk and pulled it toward him.

"Sorry about that, I didn't mean to cause you no trouble," he said quietly.

"You didn't. But I wanted to check and make sure you are okay."

He glanced up at Lucinda, who still hadn't bothered to take her eyes off her phone or pay him any attention.

"I'm okay, thank you."

"How long have you been out here?"

He sighed and leaned back against the building. There was a torn-up trash bag next to him that I assumed contained all his belongings.

"I don't even know what day it is anymore. They all start to blend together."

I nodded and pressed my lips into a thin line.

"Can I help you get to a shelter?"

"There's no room right now. I stayed there for a bit, but then they kicked me out, so I've been here ever since."

"What did you do for a living before this?"

"A little bit of everything. I've had a hard time holding down a steady job for a few years."

I took a deep breath and extended my hand to him.

"Come with me; I know somewhere you can go."

He looked at me skeptically.

"It's okay, I promise. Things are going to get better for you."

He wiped a tear from the corner of his eye and accepted my hand as I helped him to his feet.

"What's going on?" Lucinda asked, shoving her phone back into the pocket of her cut-off jean shorts.

"I'm helping a friend," I answered without looking at her.

"You *know* him?"

"No, but that doesn't mean I'm not going to help him."

"You don't have to do this," he interjected, noticing the tension coming from Lucinda.

"I know, I want to."

"I'm going to go," Lucinda threatened with her hands on her hips.

"Okay, be safe getting home." I didn't bother to watch as she turned and left, muttering *whatever* loud enough for us to hear. I helped him grab his belongings from the sidewalk and waited for him to get situated.

"Your girlfriend isn't going to be too happy," he commented, standing next to me on the sidewalk.

"She's not my girlfriend, and I'm sure she'll get over it."

He nodded, and I could tell that he was still feeling uncertain.

"My grandma has a friend who runs a rehabilitation program and houses those who need it until they can get on their feet again. We'll go see him and check if he has any open rooms."

"That's mighty kind of you, thank you."

"No problem." I smiled and started walking slowly so he could keep up with me.

"What's your name?" I asked, turning to make eye contact with him.

"Darryl. You?"

"I'm Miles."

"Nice to meet you."

"You too," I said warmly, meaning it.

"It's been a long time since anyone's paid any attention to me," he commented sadly.

"I'm sorry about that. Not everyone you meet is a good person, and not everyone is a monster, either. Guess it's just the luck of the draw."

I reflected back on the years I'd spent trying to locate my dad. At one point, he had joint custody, and I'd been living on the streets with him until my mother found out and went to court to file for full custody. Once I was old enough to look for him, I did and didn't stop until I'd found him under a bench at the bus stop. He'd been dead for days, and not a single person had bothered to check on him.

Soon, we were standing outside, waiting for Erick to answer the door.

"Sorry it's so late," I apologized when he pulled the door open. "My friend, Darryl here needs a place to stay, and the shelter is full."

"No problem, your grandma called a few minutes ago to let me know you were on your way. Come on in."

We stepped inside, and I could tell that Darryl was feeling more comfortable than he was when we first met. I hated that he had to feel so guarded around people and wondered how many times he'd asked for help and had been turned away.

"I have one room right now, and it's yours, but there are some conditions to you staying here," Erick said sternly. He was a large man, and I couldn't imagine that he'd experienced much trouble with anyone, given how intimidating he looked. My grandma had told me that he was a veteran who was focused on helping those who needed it.

"Yes, sir," Darryl answered.

"First, I don't tolerate any substance use, including alcohol, drugs, or even cigarettes. We are a clean house, and it will stay that way."

"Yes, sir."

"Second, we all help out around here. No one lives here for free. I understand you don't have any money, which is fine. But you will work to earn your keep. We have a daily list of chores, and I'll rearrange the chart to include you."

"Yes, sir."

"I understand that you've been living on the streets. I'm happy to offer you a safe place to stay and expect you'll let me know if there's anything you need until you can get back on your feet. What kind of work are you looking for?"

Darryl shrugged and looked away bashfully.

"Are you any good in the kitchen?" I asked gently.

"Oh yeah, I used to make a mean club sandwich. Piled that sucker so high, my mama could barely get it to fit in her mouth," he laughed. "I've never cooked professionally, but my mama taught me how and I used to take care of her before she passed. After that, the bank took her house, and I didn't have anywhere to go."

I smiled softly and patted him on the back.

"I'm sorry for your loss."

"Thank you."

"Me too," Erick added.

"Darryl, if you'd like, I have a food truck and could use some help. It'd be in the evenings, which would give you time during the day to work on the items that Erick needs help with. I can't offer much but can start you at fifteen dollars an hour. You'll help with food prep before we open and then with taking orders throughout the night. Occasionally, I might ask you to help with cooking, but we'll play that by ear. What do you say?"

"I'd be honored to work for you, sir."

We shook hands, then I left him with Erick to get settled in. I headed home, feeling on top of the world for being able to help someone in need.

As I got back to my house, I felt my phone buzz and pulled it out to see my grandmother calling. It was late, but obviously, she was still up and likely wanted to ask about what had happened with Lucinda.

"Hello, Grandma," I answered and closed the door behind me.

Nine

Kat

Monday morning, I'd been anxious all day, knowing that Miles would be there when I got to work. I knew that I shouldn't let it bother me as much as it did, but he did something to me, and the resolve that I'd had against him started to waver.

While I didn't know Miles personally, I knew men like him. Good-looking, flirty, the kind of personality that drew people in just so they could get what they wanted. I'd been burned plenty of times in my short twenty-eight years, and very few of those occurred in the kitchen.

I'd slept like shit last night; my nerves were shot, and a knot in my stomach made it difficult to get comfortable. I stopped by my favorite little coffee shop on my way to Ambrosia and asked for a double shot of espresso—I was going to need it today.

When I got there, I hoped I would be the first one to arrive but was disappointed when I found the door unlocked and Clarissa upfront at the hostess station. If she was already there, there was a good chance that Miles was too.

"Hey," she said casually as she thumbed through the papers in front of her. "Early again."

"I wanted to get a head start."

She looked up and smiled.

"Or were you worried that he'd be here before you and invade your space?"

I narrowed my eyes at her and took a sip of my coffee.

"You're the one who invited him here to invade it in the first place."

"Yes, but you guys are the ones who came up with this competition. I was just giving you a location to have it and wanted it to be fair. Imagine if you were thrown into his arena and had no idea where things were."

"Fine," I rolled my eyes, earning a laugh from her. "Is he back there?" I lifted my to-go cup toward the kitchen.

She shrugged and then picked up the phone that started ringing.

Sighing, I pushed my purse up my shoulder and made my way to the back.

I was relieved when I didn't see him and hung my purse and coat by the door. As I turned around, coffee in hand, I almost spilled it all over myself when I saw him walking past casually.

"Sorry, didn't mean to startle you," he said with a wink.

I tried to smile, but it fell flat, so I headed to my station and set the cup down before I had a chance to spill it again.

"So, is there anything special you're working on today?" he asked, stirring whatever he was making in the pot on the stove. I didn't want to admit it, but it smelled fantastic.

"I have a few ideas I want to flesh out."

I kept my head down and focused as I tried to remember what those ideas were. It was like having Miles around put me in this fog, and I couldn't think straight.

I grabbed my phone, opened the app where I'd kept all my recipe ideas, and thumbed through them until I found the one I was looking for. I nodded and went to the walk-in freezer to get what I needed.

I heard the door open a few minutes later as Miles walked in.

I glanced at him and then turned back to look through the meat options. Just as I reached for a cut of pork, I felt his arm brush against mine as he grabbed the one next to me.

"Sorry," he apologized, not bothering to move his arm as the electricity sparked between us.

I wanted nothing more than to turn into his body and kiss him, but I knew I couldn't. He was dangerous and had *heartbreaker* written all over him. From the tattoos that stretched up his muscular arm to the piercing green eyes that were fixated on me, I found it hard to walk away.

I knew he was attracted to me; he'd made that much clear already. What I didn't expect was how attracted to him I would be. Being this close to his body was detrimental, and I needed to move away, but my feet refused to oblige.

He grabbed a rack of ribs and pulled away, watching me with curiosity.

"Did you need help?" he asked, nodding to the pork loin I was still touching.

"No," I whispered, looking for the anger that usually resided so close to the surface when I was around him. That dream had really done me in the other night.

"Okay." He took his meat and left me alone in the cold freezer where I belonged until I cooled off a bit.

I came out a few minutes later, keeping my chin tucked as I avoided looking at him. He was busy slathering a sauce from the pot onto the ribs, slowly gliding the brush along every inch in the most seductive way—or maybe I just imagined that was what his hand would look like as he touched me.

I shook my head, forced the thoughts away, and got to work on my dish.

An hour later, Clarissa came back to check in with us. I talked to her about the herb-crusted stuffed pork loin dish I'd created.

"This looks and smells delicious," she commented before cutting a piece and taking a bite. She closed her eyes and moaned while she chewed. "Miles, come here; you have to taste this."

I felt my shoulders stiffen as he walked over, smiling broadly before opening his mouth to accept the bite she offered him off the new fork she'd grabbed.

He kept his eyes on me while he chewed, lifting a finger to wipe his mouth in a way that had my insides tingling.

"What do you think?" Clarissa asked.

"Perfection."

I smiled nervously, feeling the weight of his gaze still on me.

"I'd like to add it to the menu this week," Clarissa announced. "Do you think you can have this ready to go by Thursday?"

"Absolutely." I smiled and held my head proudly.

After she left and went back up front, I sat down at my desk in the back and made a list of ingredients we'd need on the next order.

Soon after, the staff started filling the kitchen as Miles said goodbye and left to work the food truck. I took a deep breath and slowly let it out, determined to be more focused than I was on Saturday.

Ten

Miles

I spent most of the night getting Darryl set up but was relieved when he caught on quickly and didn't need much guidance after that. I didn't need to explain to Anthony why he was there. He knew me well enough to know that I was helping someone out and was immediately on board.

We were busy for a Monday night, but nothing compared to how busy Ambrosia was. I itched to go back inside and watch Kat in her element but refrained from it tonight. I couldn't help but wonder if I was the reason they'd had a rough night on Saturday. I also could feel the tension in her body every time I was near her and knew that she was fighting the attraction that flowed so easily between us.

But with Kat, I wasn't going to rush anything. I wanted her to figure out what she wanted and then act on it, even if that meant I had to wait forever. Pushing her into it would only lead to her regretting it and pushing me even further away. No matter how hard I'd tried, I couldn't walk away from her without knowing what this thing between us was, so I wasn't willing to risk it by being impatient.

While the night progressed on, Darryl and Anthony took over the orders while I sat back and looked through some menu options I'd been playing around with for the competition. I had no idea what I wanted to make, I just knew I wanted to impress Kat. For no reason other than I desperately wanted her attention, anyway I could get it. Did that make me sound like a loser? Maybe. Did I care? No.

I was lost in thought when I heard a slight commotion at the window. I set my notepad down and got up to see what was happening.

"It's you," a feminine voice commented, making Darryl pull back from the window.

Anthony leaned forward, his large frame blocking most of the window.

"Do you know each other?"

I could hear the protective tone in his voice and relaxed.

"We don't know each other per se, but Miles and I ran into him last night. I didn't expect to see him *here*."

I watched as Darryl's shoulders slumped. I clapped a hand on his shoulder, pulling his attention to me.

"Hey, why don't you take a break? You've earned it. I'll take this one."

He nodded and stepped aside as I took my place next to Anthony.

"Lucinda," I said dryly. "What can I get for you?"

Her face lit up as she saw me, her attitude completely changing.

"How about a do-over of our date last night?" She batted her thick lashes at me.

I leaned down, watching her eyes as they lingered on my biceps as my t-shirt clung to my body.

"That wasn't a date, Lucinda."

She pouted her mouth and frowned.

"My grandma asked me to show you around town, maybe help you make some new friends, but that was it."

"Well, we didn't get very far, did we? I think your grandma

might be disappointed if she knew how the night ended."
She puffed out her chest defiantly.

I rubbed my thumb across my jaw and looked around before
answering her.

"My grandma is aware of how the night ended. She's also
aware that I stopped to help someone in need while you
played on your phone before leaving."

For a brief second, I could swear that I saw guilt or shame
flash across her face, but then it was gone.

"Well, you had it handled, so it wasn't like you needed me."

"No, I didn't need you," I agreed. "But it would have been
nice if you had *wanted* to stick around and help."

"So you're punishing me for not being there? How was I
supposed to know that was what you expected of me?"

I stood up and folded my arms over my chest.

"You weren't. But that's the difference between us, Lucinda,
and why I'm not interested in hanging out. I want to do good
in the world. Help people who need it. I don't want to be
around people who can walk by and ignore it unless someone
tells them to stop. We're two different people, that's all."

"Well," she huffed. "You're making a huge mistake. Guys are
constantly trying to get with me." She jutted her chin out.

"That's great, you won't have any problems finding
someone new to hang out with."

I winked as she glared at me before turning and storming off.

Anthony chuckled and sat down next to Darryl, sitting
sheepishly in the corner, sipping a bottle of water.

I looked down at my watch and realized he hadn't had
anything to eat since we'd been open almost five hours ago.

"How about I make us some dinner while it's slow?" I asked both of them.

"Sounds good, want some help?" Anthony offered.

"Na, I'm good. Anything you guys feel like?"

Tonight had been a sandwich night which made it easy with little prep. While I'd convinced myself that it was to help Darryl get adjusted, part of me knew that I'd picked an easy menu because I'd spent too much time at Ambrosia with Kat.

"I'll take a BLT," Anthony answered, looking to Darryl. "What do you like? My man Miles can whip up anything you're in the mood for."

"I'm okay, thank you." Darryl tucked his head and peeled at the label on his water bottle.

I squatted in front of him, waiting for him to look at me.

"One of the perks of working on this food truck is enjoying the food we make. Consider it part of your employee benefits, if you will."

The corners of his lips tugged up into a smile.

"Either I can make you something, or if you'd like, you're welcome to make yourself something. You're already familiar with where everything is; feel free to help yourself."

"Okay, thank you."

I nodded and got up. I didn't want to push or make him uncomfortable, so I gave him space while I made BLTs for Anthony and me. A few minutes later, he was up behind me, making a turkey and cheese sandwich.

"Do you want to warm it up?" I asked, moving to the side, so he had room to join me.

"Sure." He smiled and put the bread into the toaster oven.

"Thank you for the sandwich."

"You're welcome."

My heart felt bigger and fuller than it had ever felt before.

54

Eleven
Kat

The rest of the week flew by quickly and was more or less uneventful, aside from the nerves I continued to feel while trying to work with Miles in the kitchen. Every day I would be a flustered mess until he left to work the food truck.

By Sunday, I'd already had my menu created for the competition, though I had no idea what Miles was preparing, so I naturally felt unprepared. It was a feeling that I hated and it helped bring back some of the anger that I needed to keep my guard up against him.

It wasn't that I wanted to hate him; it was just a lot easier to focus on that instead of the mounting attraction that continued to rise up, despite me trying to keep it away. The man was like a forbidden piece of fruit, and I wanted to devour it.

And it wasn't just that he'd kept getting in my space at work— that was bad enough, especially when he'd *accidentally* brush against me when trying to get to something in the freezer or pantry. He'd also started to wear snug-fitting t-shirts that wrapped so tightly around his body that I found it hard to concentrate. The weather was getting warmer, which meant he wasn't wearing hoodies or loose-fitting clothes that hid his body anymore. It was yet another distraction that I didn't need.

Monday, I'd gone to work, ready for another day, when I found Clarissa at the front, looking overly stressed out.

"What's wrong?" I asked, setting my coffee down.

"Apparently, there's a nasty bug going around, and we're

down two chefs tonight. We also have reservations for two eight tops, and Lauren called in, sick too."

"Okay, we can manage. What do you need from me? Do you want me to change the menu to something easier tonight?"

Clarissa exhaled heavily and was about to answer when Miles walked in.

"On second thought," she mumbled, her eyes lighting up as he walked over.

"Everything alright?" he asked, looking between us.

"I hate to ask," Clarissa said while gripping the side of the podium. "But is there any way you can fill in for Javier tonight? We're down two chefs and a server."

"Stomach flu?" he asked, pulling his face in disgust.

"Unfortunately."

"Yeah, my buddy Anthony has it too."

He looked down at his watch, then out to where the food truck was parked outside.

"If you can't, it's not a big deal. I know Anthony usually helps you, so you're in a bind, too," Clarissa said softly.

"Actually, I can close the truck for the night. It's not a big deal."

"Oh, no, I couldn't ask you to do that."

"It's not a problem at all. And, I might be able to help with the shortage here, too. I have a friend, Darryl, who's been helping me out with the truck. He should be there in an hour, but if you're okay with it, I can ask him to come here instead. I pay him fifteen an hour, so if you could match that, I know he would appreciate it."

"What kind of work?"

"He does prep for me but has a lot of kitchen experience. I've had him prepare food for me and run orders."

"Do you think he could manage the expo station for us?"

"I think he'd be the perfect fit."

I stood there watching as they continued their conversation without me.

"Perfect. If you want to let him know to come in a little early, I'll have him complete some paperwork and get him set up. Pay is twenty-two an hour as my thank you for him coming to help at the last minute."

"I'll let him know."

"You're the best."

She smiled, took the stack of papers with her, and headed to her office.

"It's nice of you to help out," I commented as we walked to the kitchen together.

"It's not a problem at all."

"Yeah, but you're keeping your truck closed tonight to help us. That's huge. Not many people would do that."

"I'm not like most people."

I wanted to comment and say something like *I know, you're better than most people,* but that would mean that I had been watching him and might give him the wrong impression.

Instead of working on new menu ideas, Miles and I spent the extra time we had getting things ready for tonight. I was busy prepping the vegetables and garnish while he pulled the meats we needed to the front of the freezer and made sure each station had what they needed for the dishes we would be serving tonight.

Like always, I constantly found him in my space and couldn't help but wonder if he was doing it on purpose. We were a week away from the competition, and I was no closer to figuring out how to share a space with him.

I was standing at the counter, refilling the bottles of oil for each station, when I felt him come up behind me. He leaned in past me, resting one hand on my hip as his muscular chest pressed against my back as he reached into the tight space to grab the seasonings he needed from the shelf.

Granted, there was plenty of room on the other side of me, but he chose to squeeze into the narrow space where the counter formed an L shape.

My breath hitched in my throat as his fingers dug deeper into my skin as he extended his reach.

"Sorry," he breathed into my ear. "Just needed the cumin and paprika."

I tried to respond, but a soft moan escaped my lips instead.

I knew he could feel the way my body was betraying me because he didn't bother to pull away once he had the spices he needed.

Instead, he pressed a little harder, letting me feel the hard outline of his cock as it strained against the thick fabric of his jeans.

"This is what you do to me, Kat," he whispered. "You drive me crazy wanting to touch you."

His lips brushed against my ear, sending a shiver through me.

Just then, the kitchen doors swung open, and he stepped away.

I hung my head and tried to steady my breathing as Jamie walked in. I felt her eyes on me as she hung her stuff up on the coat rack by the door, but she didn't say anything.

Soon, the kitchen was bustling, and Clarissa was doing a quick rundown with everyone before we opened. Darryl had shown up early, impressing Miles with a new haircut and appropriate attire. I didn't know much about his story, but I could see the pride in Miles' eyes as he talked privately with him.

"Alright, guys," I said loudly, drawing everyone's attention as the first few orders came in. "Let's get this night off to a great start. I need three buffalo burgers, two shrimp scampi, and a lobster tail. Let's go!"

A collective *yes, Chef,* murmured around me as they got busy preparing the orders.

Since we had Miles helping out tonight, I felt easily distracted as I watched him work. I needed something to occupy my mind and decided to jump in and help with the cooking, leaving Jamie to check the plates after Darryl finished the final touches. Things were running smoothly until I realized that the only open space for me to work was right next to Miles.

He grinned as if knowing my predicament and scooted over to make room for me.

"Thanks," I mumbled and got situated next to him.

He smiled and flipped the skillet in his hand, shuffling the vegetables around before returning it to the stove.

We'd prepped most of what we thought we needed before we opened, but as I looked around, I realized we were already running low. I grabbed the extra from the counter behind me and got to work washing them before peeling and cutting. Before I knew it, we had a system going where, as soon as I had the next batch ready, he was plating the cooked ones and adding mine to the skillet.

It was weird to see how easily we were navigating the tight space we shared between us, but I tried not to focus on it. We were in the thick of the rush, and orders were coming in quicker than we could get them out. It'd been a while since

I'd been on the cooking side of the kitchen, and I forgot how stressful it could be.

Soon, Miles was serving food before I could prepare the next batch. I felt the pressure building as I slid my knife through a potato, feeling my hand slightly shake.

Miles looked over and noticed, then, without warning, stepped behind me to get another potato to get us caught up and gripped a hand around my waist.

I gasped sharply at the contact, bringing the knife straight down on my finger.

"Son of a bitch," I yelled, drawing the attention of everyone in the kitchen, including Clarissa, who had just come back to see how things were going.

"Chef has a severe cut," Miles announced, stepping beside me and grabbing a towel to wrap my hand.

"Take her to my office; there's a first aid kit in the cabinet by the door," Clarissa said, grabbing an apron from the rack and tying it around her waist. "Jamie, I need you to take over vegetables. I'll step in as an expediter. Let's go, everyone, stay focused; we have dishes to serve."

I moved aside and allowed Miles to lead me to the private bathroom in the back after he stopped to grab the first aid kit.

He gently unwrapped the towel and looked at my finger before placing my hand under the water.

I hissed at the burning sting and closed my eyes.

"You cut it pretty good, but I don't think you need stitches," he said quietly while he held it in place.

"It's all your fault," I muttered, keeping my eyes closed while he turned off the water and laid my hand on the edge of the sink.

"My fault? How's it my fault?"

He opened the first aid kit and dug around until he found what he needed.

"Because you keep touching me, and every time you do, I get all…"

I sighed, letting my words drop off.

I felt pressure against my finger as he squeezed some ointment on it and then wrapped a layer of gauze around it.

"I get you all what?" he asked, his voice gruffer than it was a few minutes ago.

"Nothing."

He tore a piece of tape off and wrapped it around the bandage. Then he pulled away, and I opened my eyes to find him leaning against the wall, studying me with his arms folded over his chest.

"Thanks for your help," I said, lifting my hand as I stood up and stepped toward the door. He stayed where he was but kept his gaze locked on me.

"I can help with the other problem, too," he said casually.

I turned and looked at him, confused by what he meant.

"The frustration." He pushed off the wall, licking his lips as he crowded my space again.

I sucked in a ragged breath, feeling the heat from his body as he stood inches away from me.

"I'm fine," I lied, refusing to meet his eyes.

"Is that why you keep dropping things and seem to lose focus when I'm around? Because I'm pretty sure I'm having the same effect on you that you're having on me."

"I don't know what you're talking about." My breathing was

shallow as all the blood drained from my body and went straight to my clit.

He took another step forward, gently pushing me against the wall with his fingers against my stomach.

"Are you sure about that?" He tilted his head to the side and placed his leg between mine as he leaned closer. "I'll back off if you want me to, just say the word, Kat. If not, let me help you with that frustration."

"I'm fine," I panted softly, hating that my body was betraying me.

The truth was, I wanted nothing more than for him to release some of this pent-up sexual frustration that I was feeling. I wanted to ride him into the sunset.

"Okay," he replied quietly, stepping away from me.

I immediately missed the close proximity of his body next to mine but fought the urge to reach out and grab him by his shirt and pull him back to me.

"You ready to get back out there?"

I tried to focus on his words, but they wouldn't register in my head. All I could think about was the aching between my thighs and how wet my panties were.

"What?" I asked after a few minutes of him staring at me with lust-filled eyes.

"We should get back out there unless you want to take me up on my offer."

My eyes lifted to find his, and I knew he knew right then and there what I wanted.

He leaned forward and cupped the side of my face with his hand as he rested his forehead against mine.

"Why are you fighting this so hard, Kat?" he breathed.

"Because I know guys like you," I whispered. "They always want one thing, and then once they get it, they're gone."

"What makes you so sure you know me? I've never asked for anything from you. I'm literally standing in the bathroom, begging you to let me touch you so I can make you come, Kat. I don't want anything other than to watch your face as you come on my hand, my tongue, or whatever you want. You need a release, and I want to give it to you."

His hand dropped from my face and slowly caressed my arm before moving to my stomach.

"I don't want anything in return," he promised and let his hand hover over the button on my dress slacks. "I just want you to feel good."

I swallowed hard, feeling drunk on his words.

"Okay," I panted, lifting my hips to allow his fingers to graze my pussy. "But just this once."

"Good girl," he murmured against my ear. "Use me for your pleasure. Fuck my hand; show me what you want. Tell me what you need to get off, Kat."

"Touch me," I begged, pressing his hand firmly against me. "Use your fingers."

While I wasn't opposed to him eating me out, we didn't really have time for that, nor was the bathroom big enough. He nudged my head to the side and kissed my neck while his hands worked to undo the button, then slid the zipper down on my pants.

I leaned my head against the wall as his fingers pushed the fabric down my hips enough for him to get the access that he needed. He continued kissing me, going up one side and then the other. I grabbed the back of his neck, desperate to feel him closer.

Then he flattened his palm and slid his hand into my panties.

"Spread your legs," he commanded, pushing them further apart with his leg.

I did as he asked and then gasped when I felt a finger slide through my wet folds.

I bit my lip to keep from crying out. My body was on fire, every touch more intense and amplified.

"God, you're so fucking wet," he growled. "I'm going to make you come in seconds, Kat."

"Do it," I panted.

My chest rose and fell heavily as he slid another finger inside and pumped faster.

"I could do this all day," he whispered. "The things I want to do to your body if we had the time. I could make you feel real good, baby. I bet you're a squirter, aren't you?"

He kept talking, his dirty words turning me on even more.

"Fuck," I cried when he began rubbing my clit with his thumb while continuing to fuck me with his fingers.

I felt the tingling sensation crawl up my spine as I got close to an orgasm.

Just then, there was a knock on the door.

"How's it going in there?" Clarissa asked.

My eyes bulged as I clasped a hand over my mouth and tried to push Miles away. A wicked smile spread across his face as he kept going, not budging from his place between my legs.

"We're good. Kat's real close to coming," he replied naturally.

I smacked him with my other hand before letting my eyes roll back in pleasure as he rubbed my clit harder.

"She's coming out in just a minute," he corrected.

"Okay, just wanted to make sure she was okay."

He increased the pressure, and suddenly my orgasm crashed over me as Clarissa stood on the other side of the door. It was surprisingly arousing to know that she was standing there, and if I weren't quiet, she would know that I was coming. The thought of someone catching us sent me even more over the edge as I spasmed against his fingers, my pussy clenching so tightly that my knees almost buckled, and I had to hold onto his shoulders to keep from falling.

"Good girl," he whispered. "Such a tight little pussy."

I was still panting, trying to catch my breath as I heard her footsteps as she walked away.

Beads of sweat dotted my brow as I tried to right myself after Miles pulled his fingers out of me and then washed his hands.

I didn't know what to say. My body felt better than it ever had, but my mind was racing, letting me know all of the reasons why I shouldn't have allowed that to happen.

"You okay?" he asked with a brow raised while he dried his hands.

I nodded, not entirely sure I believed myself.

"We should get back out there before Clarissa gets suspicious."

"Right," I agreed, sucking in a deep breath as I pulled my zipper up and buttoned my pants. I glanced in the mirror, making sure no one could tell what had just happened. Did it show that I'd just had a mind-blowing orgasm? It didn't matter. I couldn't hide in here forever, so I pulled my shoulders back and led the way back to the kitchen.

<u>Twelve</u>
Miles

I couldn't help but notice the change in Kat as we returned to the kitchen and tried to act like I hadn't just finger fucked her in the bathroom a few minutes before.

She was much more relaxed, and there was a nice color on her cheeks that made my dick stir with excitement because I knew why it was there.

I resumed my position, relieving Jamie as she joined Kat at the front of the kitchen. Everything was running smoothly, and I was happy to see Darryl keeping up with the flow. The night was winding down, but I knew we still had another hour or so of a full-on rush, so I kept my head down and stayed focused.

Clarissa had popped in a few times, and I noticed the curious glances she'd given to Kat and me but chose to ignore them. The last thing I wanted to do was draw attention to Kat and make her feel embarrassed about what happened.

"I need two cheesecakes, one lava cake on the fly," Jamie announced to the pastry chef.

I looked up to find her whispering in Kat's ear as she hung the ticket on the rack. Kat's eyes lifted to mine, and a blush spread across her face as she shook her head no and looked away. Jamie glanced at me, then turned her focus on the remaining orders that needed to go out.

"How's it going?" Clarissa asked, standing next to me as I cut more vegetables and tossed them into the pan. It was the last two dinner orders that we had, and I was ready to be done.

"Great," I smiled at her and finished cutting the last few potatoes.

"Thanks for taking care of Kat." She leaned against the cabinet behind her and looked around the kitchen. If she only knew *just how well* I'd taken care of Kat. "And thank you for being here tonight. You were a lifesaver. Darryl too."

"He's a great guy," I replied, steering the compliments to where they were needed. "Just trying to get a fresh start. I appreciate you giving him a chance tonight."

"He ran a few plates out for us early when we were in the weeds. Didn't have to think twice, he was a complete natural."

"I can tell." I smiled proudly at him.

"I know he's been working for you, and I don't want to overstep, but if he's ever looking for another job, I'd love to bring him on here."

"His employment with me is temporary until he gets on his feet again. I think he'd appreciate the offer if you want to make it."

She nodded and squeezed my shoulder.

"Thank you, I'll be sure to do so before he leaves tonight."

Once she was gone, I finished cooking the veggies, plated them, and sent them to the warming station until the meat was ready. I took off my apron and hung it behind me, officially done for the night, aside from cleaning up.

Kat took the lead on getting the last few orders out while Jamie jumped in to help with the dishes. I loved that no one in the kitchen felt above anyone else and that they all joined in to get the job done. I had worked in a few kitchens before starting the food truck and knew that it was rare to have such a strong bond between employees. Typically you find everyone looking out for themselves and not worrying about others. That pushed me out of those environments and led me to start my own business.

After everyone had left, Kat and I were the last two left. She'd stuck around to work on the menu for the next day while I'd stuck around to spend time with her. I found stuff to clean, so it wasn't overly obvious, but my goal was to see if she'd let me take her home again, or better yet, out for a bite to eat so we could talk.

It was after eleven when Kat finished and slipped her purse over her shoulder. I could see the exhaustion on her face and knew tonight wasn't the night to try to hang out. But I couldn't help but feel the need to check in and see how she felt after what had happened earlier.

I grabbed my stuff and was ready to head out with her when Clarissa came back.

"Can I talk to you two for a moment?" she asked.

Kat's face fell, and I knew she was worried that Clarissa knew what had happened between us in the bathroom.

"Sure, what's up?" I said, breaking the silence.

"I've found three food bloggers who are interested in judging the competition next weekend, as well as Luka Fagiolo from The Starling."

"That's great," I replied, noticing how nervous she seemed.

"It is," she agreed, nodding her head. "One of them asked how we would feel about having the event recorded. He has a friend who works for one of the local news channels, and they thought this would be a fun story to cover. I wanted to run the idea by both of you first as I know this was supposed to be a fun, friendly competition, and I don't want to overstep by allowing the press to get involved and broadcast it."

Kat chewed her lip nervously.

"I'll give you two time to talk about it. You don't have to decide tonight, but with the competition only being a week away, I do need to give them an answer by Wednesday."

"Okay, we'll discuss it and let you know."

"Thanks, and great job tonight. See you guys tomorrow."

I walked with Kat into the brisk evening air and waited for her to say something, but she didn't.

"Are you okay?" I asked, gently touching her elbow to get her attention.

"Yeah, I'm just processing the info."

"It's a lot to think about."

"It's not just that," she sighed, leaning against the side of the building. "I've always dreamed of being a chef at The Starling, working under and learning from Luka. It makes me nervous that he will be one of the judges."

"The nice thing is that it's just a fun competition. There's no pressure to impress anyone," I tried to reassure her.

She pulled away from the wall and shook her head at me.

"You don't get it. Luka remembers everyone. If he comes to judge this and I mess it up, it'll kill any chance I have of ever working in his kitchen. He can literally end my career with one bad comment. A negative review could tarnish the reputation I've worked so hard to build."

"Shit," I mumbled, scrubbing a hand down my jaw. "Do you want me to talk to Clarissa and see if she can find someone else?"

"No," she said sadly. "You don't cancel on Luka. I just have to try my best not to screw this up."

She turned and walked away. What was supposed to be a fun competition between us had now spiraled into something heavier and more intense than I'd ever imagined.

Thirteen

Kat

Tuesday and Wednesday were easier with Miles not coming into work since he needed to focus on the food truck while Anthony was still sick. Clarissa had reached out to a friend who had two bored teenagers who needed more spending money, so they'd come in and helped in the kitchen with basic stuff, like dishes and prep work, until everyone recovered from the stomach bug that was going around.

I'd felt stressed out that the competition was right around the corner, and I had less than a week to finish preparing for it. What was supposed to be a fun, lighthearted way to shut Miles up had turned into something huge and terrifying for me, knowing that Luka would be judging it.

I'd gotten to Ambrosia Thursday afternoon before Miles and was busy working on the menu for next week when he'd walked in.

"Hey," he said happily, sending my heart pitter-pattering in my chest.

"Hi."

His brows furrowed slightly at my tone as he went to his station and set his stuff down.

"Everything alright?"

"Fine." I kept my head down and tried to remember what I was supposed to be doing.

I tried taking slow, soothing breaths to help calm me,

but when he stood beside me and I felt his gaze on me, it stopped working.

"Kat," he said more as a warning than my name.

"What?" I refused to look up at him. I wrote down a bunch of random notes, not sure that I'd have any idea what they were supposed to mean later when I felt his hand close over mine to stop me.

"What's going on?"

"Nothing, I'm just busy." Giving up, I dropped the pen and pulled my hand out of his grasp. I tried to keep the emotion off my face, but as his eyes searched my face, I knew he could read me.

"Bullshit."

"Excuse me?" I folded my arms over my chest and tilted my head.

"I said that's bullshit. Something is wrong, I can see it all over your face."

"You don't know me well enough to read my mood from my face."

"I know you better than you think."

He kept his spot next to me and leaned a hip against the counter, effectively pinning me in the corner again. Why did he always have to find a way to trap me in such close proximity?

"Now I'm calling bullshit," I snorted but felt my neck tingle as a blush crept up as he lifted a finger and rubbed it across his bottom lip. My eyes were laser-focused on the action as my body betrayed me again and leaned slightly toward him.

He waited me out for a few minutes, playing with his lip as if it didn't have a catastrophic impact on me. He knew it did, I could see it in his eyes as they lit up every time I watched him.

"Is this about what happened on Monday?" he asked gently.

I rolled my eyes and shook my head.

"That's what I thought."

"Because you just happen to know everything?" I bit out sarcastically.

"More than you think."

"Okay, fine, yes, I'm upset about what happened on Monday. There, are you happy?"

"Why are you upset about it?"

I threw my hands in the air as my eyes widened at him. Why wouldn't I be? He was there, he knew what had happened. It had repeatedly been playing in my head ever since, and the guilt of what I'd done had been eating away at me.

"Why wouldn't I be? It was completely irresponsible and reckless of me to do that."

"Why?"

"Because we're not dating, and I let you finger me in the bathroom like it was no big deal. On top of that, I let my team down. We were in the middle of a rush, and instead of being out here to support them, I was hiding in the bathroom doing dirty stuff!"

He pushed his lips together and watched me.

"You're feeling guilty over two things that you shouldn't. First—your team was just fine. You saw that for yourself when we came back, and nothing had fallen apart. I love that you're a team player and wanted to help out, but you also weren't in any headspace to be helpful to them. You were wound so tight that you were distracted—hence your finger almost getting cut off."

"But—"

He held his hand up to stop me.

"Second, there is absolutely no reason you should feel upset or ashamed over what happened in the bathroom, Kat. We are two adults who consented to what happened. Do you not deserve to have pleasure?"

I pulled my head back and frowned.

"Yes, but—"

"No buts, Kat. Either you believe you deserve to have pleasure, or you don't. My point is that you shouldn't feel ashamed if it was something you wanted. Women are highly sexual beings, and I love that about them. Just because society says that you shouldn't be allowed to seek it out without feeling shameful for it doesn't mean that you have to do what society says."

My jaw dropped open as he talked.

"And for the record," he whispered and leaned closer. "You look fucking gorgeous when you come. There's nothing to be embarrassed about. You wanted pleasure, and I gave it to you, simple as that."

He pulled back and raised his brows at me.

"I can't tell you to stop feeling guilt over these things, but I can assure you that I feel it's misplaced, and maybe you're focusing on feeling guilty because it's easier than allowing yourself to admit that you might have felt something when I touched you."

"I—" I shook my head and snapped my jaw shut. It was like he had some magic spell on me, and I couldn't think straight.

What he said made sense, but it wasn't that easy to just give up the guilt that I'd felt and embrace the power he was talking about. What would it feel like to have sex with someone simply because I wanted to be fucked and not worry about what people would think if they found out? My mom's voice echoed far off in the depths of my mind, reminding me of how a lady should act and being openly sexual, wasn't it.

Plus, it was true, I had felt something when he touched me, and I hadn't stopped thinking about since. Even when I'd slipped my hand into my panties last night to deal with the lingering frustration I felt from wanting him to touch me again. I'd imagined it had been his hand instead of mine, and that thought alone had me coming in seconds.

"Being attracted to me isn't such a terrible thing," he said, pushing away. "And just for the record, I could make you feel ten times better than I did the other night. Consider that a preview."

He winked and walked over to his station, getting ingredients together as if nothing had just happened between us.

Fourteen

Miles

Darryl and I had knocked it out of the park tonight with the food truck. He was a quick learner and had already figured out what we needed before I had to ask.

The night wound down, and I was cleaning up when I saw Clarissa leaving Ambrosia. She looked over at me, then headed my way.

"I feel like all I ever do is ask you for favors," she laughed. "But I have another one."

"What's up?" I stopped wiping the counter and gave her my full attention.

"I need to pick my in-laws up from the airport, so that leaves Kat alone. I don't feel comfortable having her leave alone and was wondering if you might be able to check on her and maybe hang out until she gets to her car safely?"

"Not a problem at all."

"She was finishing up a few minutes ago, so I don't expect she'll be long."

I gave her a nod and then turned to Darryl when she left.

"We're just about done if you want to take off," I offered. "I'm going to stick around to make sure Kat gets home okay."

"Sounds good, boss."

He finished what he was doing and then left. I closed the food truck and knocked on the door to Ambrosia.

A few minutes later, Kat came out, glancing nervously at the door until she saw me.

"What are you doing here?" she asked after unlocking and opening it for me.

"Clarissa said you were closing by yourself, so I came to check on you."

"I told her I was fine," she grumbled and walked back to the kitchen.

I followed after making sure that I locked the door behind me.

"I need to finish a few things, and then we can go. Not that you have to stay to begin with."

Her hair was down while she sat at the desk, entering something into the computer.

I waited off to the side to keep from making her feel rushed.

"Have you decided what you're making for the competition on Sunday?" I asked, sitting on the counter.

"Yeah, but I keep second-guessing my choices," she laughed, shutting off the computer and getting up from the desk. "What about you?"

I shrugged, trying not to check her out, but it was hard. Almost as hard as my cock every time I remembered how she pulsed against my fingers the other day.

"I have a few ideas, but nothing set in stone."

She pulled her brows together and stepped toward me.

"You've talked a lot of shit about how good of a chef you are," she scolded playfully. She was almost standing between my legs, so I subtly opened them wider in case she wanted an invitation. "Don't disappoint."

"I never disappoint," I replied gruffly, noticing the sharp breath she took when she picked up on the innuendo I'd thrown out.

"Is that so?"

"I can prove it."

Her hands trembled as she let them fall to my knees.

"Show me," she whispered.

"Are you sure?"

She looked up, and locked eyes with me then nodded.

I hopped off the counter, taking up the narrow space between it and where she stood.

Without asking for permission, I grabbed the back of her head and pulled her to me as my mouth crashed down over hers.

A small whimper escaped her lips as they opened, allowing my tongue to explore. Her hands wrapped up around my neck, clawing to get closer.

"You're fucking beautiful," I growled as I broke the kiss and allowed my palms to slide down over her ass.

She closed her eyes and groaned as I kneaded the plump flesh, grabbing handfuls of thick ass.

"What do you want tonight, Kat?" I kissed along the side of her neck before nipping the bottom of her ear.

"I want you to fuck me," she panted.

"Fuck yes," I groaned, spinning her around to face the counter I'd been sitting on.

With her back pressed against my chest, I slipped my hand

down the front of her pants and into her panties, earning a gasp as I felt the warm wetness at my fingertips.

"You're so wet for me."

"Mmhmm."

"I'm going to make you feel so good, baby."

She arched her back as I slipped my fingers inside and fucked her for a few minutes. It was too hard to focus on her clit in this position, and I wanted to make sure that her orgasm was even better than the other night.

I pulled my hand out, chuckling at the way she grumbled and cursed under her breath.

"You'll be coming in a minute, don't worry," I assured her as I unbuttoned her pants and slid the zipper down. I helped her as she stepped out of them. She stood there in her thong panties and the crisp white button-down shirt, looking so fucking sexy.

She looked at me over her shoulder and chewed her lips as she waited for me to unzip my jeans and pull my cock out. I grabbed a condom out of my wallet and quickly covered myself, giving my dick a few long strokes as she watched.

Her eyes widened in surprise, and I knew she'd seen my Prince Albert piercing. She licked her lips and continued to stare.

"You ready?" I asked as I guided her over the counter and pulled her hips back so her ass popped in the air for me. Then I pushed her panties to the side, grinning when I saw how ready she was for me.

She nodded and whimpered as I reached around and rubbed her clit with my middle finger before sliding my cock inside her.

"Ahhhhhh," she moaned, letting her head hang down as I pushed slowly inside her. The counter was low enough that she could comfortably bend over it and hold onto the edge across from her as I started to fuck her faster.

Her legs were spread wide, taking my cock easily as I glided in and out of her. I continued to rub her clit and felt her body tensing as she got close.

I pumped faster and harder, tilting my hips so my dick hit her g-spot with each thrust. She cussed like a sailor as her knuckles turned white from trying to hold on while I fucked her.

"Right there," she panted. "Oh, God, right there. Don't stop. Harder."

I panted along with her, feeling my balls tighten as I grew closer to coming.

I did as she asked and continued to hit the spot that was driving her wild, both with my cock and my fingers. Soon I felt her body spasm around me and allowed my orgasm to crash through me.

Her legs were wobbly as I pulled out of her a few minutes later, but she seemed fine as she bent down to pull her pants back up.

I pulled my jeans up and went to the bathroom to dispose of the condom. When I returned to the kitchen, she was standing next to the counter we'd just fucked on, her face flushed and her body looking more relaxed than I'd ever seen.

"You okay?" I asked cautiously, noticing the uncertainty in her eyes.

She nodded.

"I wasn't expecting it to be that good," she giggled, covering her mouth with her hand.

I grinned and pulled my bottom lip between my teeth.

"You're easy to impress then. Imagine what I could do if we weren't in a hurry and had an actual bed?" I wiggled my brows.

"I guess we'll just have to try that next."

I pulled my head back in surprise.

"So you're saying there's going to be a next time?"

"Maybe?" she tossed over her shoulder before grabbing her things and leading me to the door.

Fifteen

Kat

By Saturday, I was a blundering ball of nerves and anxious about the cook-off being only a day away. I'd spent the entire morning reviewing my menu choices, wondering if it was too late to change my mind.

Ambrosia was a bustling mix of workers getting ready for the evening rush as well as preparing for the competition. Clarissa knew how distracted I was already, so she'd asked Jamie to step in as head chef for the night and sent me to go help with the prep work.

Miles was there too—of course, he was—and I found it still hard to focus with him around. Even though I'd hoped I could fuck him out of my system, it felt like he'd gotten even further under my skin, which was a distraction I couldn't afford right now.

Darryl and Anthony were running the food truck now that Anthony had recovered from his stomach bug, while Miles discussed the setup for tomorrow night and where to set the four judges. Knowing that Luka would be there made me even more nervous than I had been.

I sat at the desk and made a list of the ingredients I needed for tomorrow, knowing that I would work better if I had a checklist for each item. Lists were my thing; they kept me focused and calm. Two things that I desperately needed right now.

"How's it going?" Clarissa asked, sitting on the corner of the desk and folding her hands in her lap.

I tossed the pen down and leaned back.

"I'm so stressed about tomorrow," I admitted, catching her eye.

"Don't be; it's supposed to be fun. Remember?" She tilted her head and smiled.

"I think we threw the idea of fun out the window once you announced that Luka Fagiolo was going to be a guest judge."

Clarissa waved her hand as if it were no big deal.

"He's excited to do it," she insisted. "Plus, he owes me a favor."

My eyes bulged, and my jaw dropped.

"What?" I stuttered. "You know Luka Fagiolo?"

She nodded, clearly amused by my reaction.

"*The* Luka Fagiolo? From The Starling?"

She laughed and nodded again.

"Yes, *the* Luka Fagiolo. Though I gotta admit, it's kind of weird to keep hearing him referred to by his full name."

"How do you know him?" I asked, genuinely curious.

"We grew up together." She shrugged.

"That's it?!" I shrieked. "I've been working for you for five years, and you've never once mentioned that you happen to know THE BIGGEST chef in Seattle."

"It's not that big of a deal."

"Clarissa—he has restaurants across the country where people kill themselves just to get a job. He has a culinary school in Paris. He was a celebrity judge on the food show—what's the name of it? Oh yeah, A Cut Above. He's a big deal to most people; I don't understand how you can be so unaffected by him."

I was still trying to process the information that had just landed in my lap when Clarissa got up and smoothed down the front of her skirt.

"Yeah, well, he may be amazing with the culinary stuff, but he was a terrible boyfriend."

I didn't think it was possible, but my jaw dropped even further.

"You dated Luka?"

"For a few years."

"Why would you invite your ex-boyfriend to come be a guest judge for a random cook-off?"

"Because, like you said, he's a big deal in the culinary world, and I knew it would be good exposure for us.

She walked away and left me an even bigger mess than I was before she came over.

Sixteen

Miles

I leaned against the counter while Clarissa explained the plan for the competition to everyone for what felt like the hundredth time. I knew she was excited about it, but I couldn't help but feel like there was more riding on this than what she was letting on. What had started out as a fun, friendly way to get Kat to agree to go out with me had quickly spiraled into an all-out event that the city was buzzing over.

The kitchen had been converted into a friendly space for the four judges to sit at a large table covered in a freshly pressed linen tablecloth. There were no floral arrangements or fuss, just a clean table, free of distraction so they could watch us work.

Their table was directly across from the two stations that had been set up for Kat and me, which were already stocked with the list of ingredients and spices we had requested. The walk-in freezer had also been rearranged so our stuff was neatly organized toward the front for easy access. While this wasn't supposed to be as formal as those reality shows you saw on TV, it was starting to have that same vibe.

"The judges will be here in an hour, but the team from Channel 8 News should be here any minute to start setting up. I'll handle getting them set up, but I need Ava and Charlie to stay at the hostess station to greet the judges when they get here. There have also been a handful of calls already asking about the event, so I'll need you guys to guide people to the website where it will be live streamed."

Everyone collectively agreed, then dispersed and got to work on their assigned jobs. For Kat and me, it was simply waiting for the cook-off to start. We had the easy job for now, but I could see the stress sitting on her shoulders the closer it got.

"Hey, you ready for today?" I asked, leaning against the counter beside her and bumping shoulders.

"No."

She didn't bother to look at me, just kept her gaze straight ahead to where the judges would be sitting.

"It's going to be fine," I said reassuringly but still didn't get a response.

Finally, I turned to face her and held her hands in mine.

"Kat, if you don't want to do this, we can call it off now."

Her brown eyes sparkled in the light, but a hint of sadness lay beneath.

"We can't do that."

"Sure we can. Just say the word."

She sighed and pulled her hands away.

"Clarissa already organized everything. If we pulled out of it now, it would disappoint a lot of people, including her."

"I don't give a damn about disappointing anyone. All that I care about is you and what you want, Kat."

"I just want this to be over already," she sighed and then walked over to the busser who had called her name.

I ground my jaw and headed back to my station to get ready.

Two hours later, the judges were seated across from us, watching intently as Kat and I worked on our appetizers. I'd had an elaborate menu lined up but changed my mind right before the competition started.

The food truck was closed today, so Anthony and Darryl had been there to help me. When I'd told them my last-minute changes, they scrambled to swap out the stuff I needed before anyone noticed. It wasn't like we had to get pre-approval or anything, but I didn't want the extra chaos on my side to force Kat to feel more pressured than she already was.

"Five minutes," Clarissa called out, letting Kat and me know that we needed to have our appetizers plated and on the presentation table soon.

I nodded and lowered the slotted metal spoon into the hot oil, fishing out the last zucchini bite and setting it on the paper-towel-covered plate. While I had a few minutes left, I stirred the marinara sauce I'd made from scratch and turned off the heat.

My appetizer was simple and easy to assemble on four plates for each of the judges. I carried them over to the presentation table, stood to the side, and waited for Kat to join me with her dishes. Once she set her plates down, Clarissa nodded, and the servers collected and served them.

"Alright, Kat, you're up first," Clarissa announced, standing to the side as the cameraman panned around her to get an up-close shot of Kat. "What did you prepare tonight for your appetizer?"

She swallowed hard and held her hands tightly in front of her to avoid fidgeting.

"I've prepared a prosciutto crostini with a balsamic honey glaze."

"Impressive," Clarissa noted with a warm smile. "Walk us through your dish, please."

Kat nodded and pulled her shoulders back.

"I used a loaf of Italian bread and cut it into one-inch slices, brushed it with an olive oil garlic paste, and baked for a few minutes until it was golden crisp. While that was cooling, I prepared the balsamic honey glaze. To assemble, I added a thin layer of burrata cheese, then a thin slice of prosciutto, and topped with freshly cracked pepper. Once each crostini was ready, I added the balsamic honey glaze and a thinly cut ribbon of basil.

The judges examined the food on their plates, lifting the bite-size appetizer before lifting it to their lips and whispering amongst themselves. I glanced at Kat, noticing her brow slightly furrowed as she waited for their reaction.

A few seconds later, she let out the breath she had been holding once they smiled and nodded in appreciation.

"Delicious," the female judge on the end commented.

"Simple and amazing—two of my favorite things," the guy on the end said with a wink.

That left the other female judge and Luka Fagiolo to give their feedback.

They both took another bite as everyone waited on pins and needles.

"I absolutely love it," the other woman said, wiping the corner of her mouth with a napkin.

She smiled, but I could see the anxiety etched on her face while she waited for Luka. His opinion is what mattered the most to her, and I knew that it was killing her not knowing what he thought.

She wrung her hands together, and I wanted to reach out and touch her but knew I couldn't. It wasn't the time or place for that, but I hated seeing how worked up she was over this stupid cook-off.

Finally, Luka set the rest of his crostini down and lifted his head, locking eyes with Kat.

"I'm not usually at a loss for words, but you've surprised me," he said without any hint of emotion on his face. "Well done."

Kat exhaled heavily, her shoulders relaxing as she stepped to the side to allow me to stand in the center while my appetizer was served to the judges.

"Miles, would you please do us the honor of telling us what you've prepared for your appetizer tonight?" Clarissa asked, her voice sounding like she'd been practicing saying the words on repeat for days.

"Sure," I said, clearing my throat so I didn't sound so unenthusiastic about it. "I've prepared zucchini bites with marinara sauce."

I watched the features on Clarissa's face change before she composed herself again.

"How delightful," she commented, walking over to where the judges were taking their first bites. "What inspired you to create this for your appetizer?"

I shrugged and felt Kat's eyes on me.

"It's simple and delicious," one of the judges noted.

The judges were busy dipping the fried zucchini bites into the cups of marinara that had been added to the side, but I could feel the heat on me from the two women standing closest to me.

"Clarissa is right; this is simply delightful." The woman on the end smiled and then pushed the rest of the bite into her mouth, giving me a wink as she did.

I didn't give her any reaction but stayed focused and turned my attention to the other judges. Two were busy finishing the rest of the food on their plate while Luka studied his and held it up in front of his face with his brows pulled together.

"Is everything alright?" Clarissa asked, drawing everyone's attention to him.

"Yes," he drew out slowly, continuing to study the zucchini bite. "My mother used to make these when I was a boy, and I haven't had them in years. The way this is fried is impressive. It's a perfect rectangle, each portion equally cooked without anything leaking out the sides."

He set it down on the plate and looked up at me.

"I can see that you tried to underwhelm us with a simple dish, but I think you've failed to give yourself enough credit for mastering the ability to turn a basic appetizer into something extraordinary."

I heard the whispers amongst us and knew that Kat was overthinking Luka's compliment and doubting herself.

Seventeen

Kat

Clarissa collected the judge's ratings for the first-round while Miles and I got to work preparing the main dishes. I felt blindsided when I saw what Miles had prepared for his appetizer. Was he trying to lose on purpose? I pushed the thoughts out of my head and tried to focus on the main course instead of entertaining the thoughts that wanted to consume my mind about how Miles got what he wanted from me and no longer cared about the stupid competition he'd started.

I kept myself busy, working diligently as the quail that I'd prepared roasted in the oven. I'd decided to go with a lavender balsamic vinegar and chardonnay reduction, which smelled heavenly. Once it was finished, I served it over a side of camembert cheese grits and added another drizzle of the sauce over the dish. I wiped each plate clean, set them on the serving counter, and then stepped to the side as Miles brought his plates over.

My heart hammered in my chest as I noticed that Miles had chosen another basic dish. When I'd gone into the walk-in freezer earlier, I saw the rack of lamb sitting to the side with the other items he'd requested. But what he'd prepared was bacon cheeseburgers with thinly sliced avocado and freshly made sweet potato fries with some sort of dipping sauce.

I glanced nervously at him, wondering what in the world he was up to.

"Kat, we'll start with you again," Clarissa announced, drawing my attention to her.

I straightened my spine and clasped my hands in front of me while the servers delivered the dishes.

I cleared my throat and then began speaking.

"I've prepared an oven-roasted quail glazed with a lavender balsamic vinegar and chardonnay reduction, served over camembert cheese grits."

I pulled my lips into a thin line and waited anxiously for their reactions.

The two women judging the competition closed their eyes and moaned as they chewed. Luka's face was unreadable— which was even more unnerving—while the other guy seemed to enjoy it but didn't make a big show of it.

"Alright, judges, what do you think?" Clarissa asked cheerfully as the camera guy followed her around to the judge's table.

"Incredible," one woman sighed.

The other two nodded and took another bite, murmuring something along the lines of it being delicious.

Luka swallowed his bite and wiped his mouth with a napkin before looking directly at me.

"You are quite talented, Ms. Elliott. I see why you're the executive chef at such a prestigious restaurant."

I swallowed the ball of emotion that was now lodged in my throat and smiled.

Clarissa beamed proudly at me and then shifted the focus to Miles' dish. I tried to listen as he explained the simplicity of what he'd prepared, but I couldn't stop obsessing over Luka's compliment. If I could impress him, then there was the possibility that I might be able to work for him someday, and that was mind-blowing. Studying under Luka Fagiolo was something that I'd wanted for as long as I could remember and to know that this might have put me slightly closer to that dream was equally exciting and nerve-wracking. We still had to prepare a dessert, which was not my strong suit.

Miles had finished talking while the judges eagerly devoured his food, tossing compliments his way as easily as the people who hovered around you on the Las Vegas strip, trying to give you cards with naked women on them.

I pushed the irritation out of my head and went to my station to start working on the next dish.

Everything was going well with my Honey Crisp apple pie until we got down to the last twenty minutes. I'd already baked the pie, minus the top of the crust since it was going to be thinner and a more intricate design that wouldn't take long to cook.

I'd already pulled the pie out and was letting it cool on the rack while I tried cutting out the designs. My fingers were shaky, but I'd also somehow messed up this part of the dough because it wasn't as firm as it was supposed to be and kept crumbling and breaking every time I tried to cut a design.

I didn't have time now to make another crust and bake it. This was the only crust that I had, and it was quickly turning into a mess.

I was going to lose the stupid competition and, even worse, make a bad impression on Luka when he saw that I couldn't even bake a simple apple pie.

The clock was ticking loudly in my head as my anxiety skyrocketed. I glanced at Miles to see him peacefully working as if he had no cares in the world. He stepped away from his dessert, smiled at it, then relaxed against the counter.

I was struggling to fix my mess with less than twenty minutes to spare, and he was already done and sailing through another round.

I shook my head and forced myself to be calm as I tried to cut another piece of crust. *You can do this. You HAVE to do this. Just move slowly, and don't let it break.*

"Son of a bitch," I muttered loud enough for Miles to look over at me. With his brows pulled together, he came over and stood next to me, looking at the pile of dough pieces scattered on the counter covered in flour.

"What's wrong?" he asked, shielding us from the judges.

"I was trying to do an elaborate crust design and must've missed something because this is not how it's supposed to look. It just crumbles." I pointed to them and rolled my neck, trying to ease some of the tension that was quickly mounting.

I looked up at him helplessly as Clarissa called out the fifteen-minute warning.

"Okay, it's not a big deal," he assured me, looking around the counter at the pie on the cooling rack and the mess I'd made.

"It's a huge deal. I have nothing to serve," I grumbled, suddenly feeling defeated as I tossed the towel behind me into the sink.

"Do you trust me?" he asked, looking me in the eyes.

"Yes." I spat out the answer before thinking and noticed how easily it came out. I did trust him, though he'd never given me a reason not to. It was just men in general that I didn't trust, but we didn't have time to unpack that right now.

"Okay, let's do this," he said, giving me an ear-to-ear smile that forced the corners of my lips up.

I watched in horror as he used two forks and crumbled the pie and crust together, making an absolute disaster out of the beautiful pie I'd made.

"What are you doing?" I hissed, my eyes wide in disbelief.

"You'll see." He winked and rushed to the freezer, then came back with a carton of vanilla ice cream.

I watched as he grabbed four bowls, scooped a serving of ice cream into each one, and then topped it with the pie mixture. He used a fork to pick a big slice of Honey Crisp apple to be the focal point for each bowl, then dusted them with cinnamon and wiped the inside of the bowls.

He stood back and placed his hands on his hips, smiling proudly.

"Five minutes," Clarissa called out.

"Okay, get those over to the table before you run out of time." He gave me a quick pat on the shoulder and then returned to his station to get his dish to the serving counter.

I stood there shocked for a few seconds, then got my ass in gear and rushed them over to the counter just in time. I smiled at Miles, mouthing a quick thank you before we both turned our attention to the judges.

"Kat, please tell us what you've prepared for dessert this evening," Clarissa said.

Suddenly, it occurred to me that I had no idea what to call whatever this was that Miles helped me create. I turned my head slightly toward him.

"Deconstructed Honey Crisp apple pie," he muttered quietly, keeping his head straight and barely moving his lips.

"It's, um, a deconstructed honey crisp apple pie served over vanilla ice cream and sprinkled with cinnamon on top."

The judges studied it, then nodded as they dove in. The hard part was over, so I took a deep breath and allowed myself to relax. I was finally able to listen as Miles explained his caramel cheesecake bars that he'd been serving at the food truck and were wildly popular.

A few minutes later, we returned to our stations, and Clarissa joined us while the judges talked amongst themselves, deciding on a winner for the night. The kitchen staff was huddled in the corner, equally as excited. Soon, we would know who the winner of the competition was, and I felt like that meant more to me than it should have.

Eighteen

Kat

Waiting for the results of the cook-off was unnerving, and I still had my suspicions on Miles' intention with simplifying his menu. He didn't seem stressed at all tonight, and if anything, he'd been kind of checked out through most of the competition.

Clarissa was rambling on about how much fun she'd had and how we should do it more often, but I couldn't focus on anything she was saying as I watched the judges discussing us. Every now and then, they would lean forward to talk without anyone hearing them, then pull back and look our way. I couldn't tell if it was good or bad as they all schooled their expressions and made it impossible to read them.

Finally, after what felt like forever, they motioned for Clarissa and handed her an envelope with their decision. Luka leaned closer, whispering something in her ear before getting up and leaving the room. My stomach turned, wondering if we had failed to impress him tonight.

"Alright, ladies and gentlemen, I have the results in my hot little hand. But before I get to that, I would like to say a huge thank you to our guest judges, the staff of Ambrosia, and Channel 8 News for all being here tonight."

I flexed my fingers a few times, holding my breath while I waited impatiently.

"By a unanimous vote, and after Luka Fagiolo deciding to retract his vote due to personal reasons, the winner of this cook-off is Kat Elliott." Clarissa turned and clapped for me as everyone in the kitchen joined in.

I let out a sigh of relief, but now that Luka had left, it didn't feel like it mattered much anymore. I had initially agreed to this absurd contest as a way to get back at Miles and to shut him down with his constant date proposals. But then, when Luka was mentioned, it was like this had shifted into a one-time shot at my dream, and I got so caught up in the idea of him offering me a job that I'd ignored everything else.

"Congratulations," Miles said, extending his hand as he approached me. Everyone else was off talking and cleaning up, leaving us by ourselves.

"Thank you, though I don't think that was a fair contest. Why did you do that?" I asked, folding my arms over my chest.

"Do what?"

"Throw the competition so I could win."

"I didn't. I made what I felt like at the time."

I shook my head.

"No, I don't believe that for a second. This whole thing was your idea to begin with, Miles. You wanted to prove that you were a better chef than me, but then you didn't bother trying."

He stepped closer, invading my space as I sucked in a deep breath.

"I could care less about proving myself to you as a chef, Kat," he growled, pinching the tip of my chin between his fingers and lifting my head to look at me. "This whole thing was a stupid way of trying to get your attention—nothing more than that."

He was right, and I knew that. The original deal was that if he won, I owed him a date. If I won, he'd leave me alone and stop asking me out.

"I'm sorry," I apologized, instantly feeling like shit for my outburst and accusing him of something that he didn't do. "I thought maybe you backed out on making the food you'd originally planned so I could win. I'm used to thinking the worst when it comes to men and relationships."

He stepped forward again, pinning me against the counter while the outline of his erection pressed firmly against my thigh. I glanced around, checking to see if anyone was watching us, but he didn't care.

"I'm not like other men, Kat. You don't have to keep your guard up around me, and I really wish you'd stop comparing me to them."

He shook his head, then turned and walked away. I saw him say something to Anthony and Darryl before glancing at me over his shoulder and storming off.

After he left, Clarissa came over to talk to me.

"So, how does it feel to win?" she asked excitedly.

I shrugged, unsure of how to answer. Miles had left me feeling frazzled and like a total bitch. Suddenly winning didn't feel that good.

"I thought this was what you wanted?" Her voice was softer as she realized something was wrong.

"It was, but I guess I lost sight of why I wanted to win."

"You mean it wasn't to prove Miles wrong and get him to stop chasing after you?" she laughed and arched a brow.

"No," I chuckled. "I can handle Miles."

She whistled through her teeth.

"I bet you can."

I pulled my head back in surprise and laughed, feeling the blush creep up my skin.

"What's that supposed to mean?"

"Nothing," she grinned. "But I do know that it doesn't take that long to bandage a cut finger, and you guys were gone an awfully long time in that bathroom by yourselves."

I covered my face with my hands and cringed. Had she heard us?

"Don't worry, we've all been waiting for you guys to get your heads out of your asses and finally act on it. Just don't do it in my kitchen," she warned with a finger pointed in my direction.

I didn't say anything because I didn't want her to know we already had. Instead, I shifted the conversation before she could walk away.

"So, what happened with Luka?" I prodded. "Why did he decide not to vote?"

She chewed her lip and looked around to see if anyone else was listening.

"He didn't want to vote because he's looking for an executive chef for his San Antonio location of The Starling and didn't want to hire someone he'd voted for in a competition."

My voice caught in my throat as I tried to force the words out.

"He's looking for an executive chef? And is picking someone from tonight?"

"It looks like it."

"Who? How will we know who he picked?" There were so many questions that I was desperate to get out.

"He said he'll reach out to them when he has an offer ready."

She raised her brows, then smiled and went over to say goodbye to the guest judges that were getting ready to leave.

Nineteen

Miles

I walked hurriedly down the street, trying to burn off some of the frustration from my conversation with Kat. How could she think that I'd gotten what I'd wanted from her? Couldn't she feel the attraction that still sizzled between us? Did she seriously think I'd already had my fill of her and was ready to move on?

 I was stewing over things when I heard someone call my name. I turned around and found Luka Fagiolo leaning against the brick wall with a cigarette hanging between his fingers.

"A word, please?" he asked as he pushed off the wall, tossed the cigarette to the ground, and stomped it out with the heel of his expensive designer shoe.

"What's up?" My tone was more brash than usual, but I didn't care. People may walk on eggshells around him, but I wasn't about to.

"Your cooking tonight impressed me."

"Thanks," I replied dryly, looking over my shoulder to see if Kat had left yet.

"You're not much into the compliments, are you?" He laughed and cocked his head to the side. His accent was thicker than I had remembered hearing earlier, though he hadn't spoken much then either.

"I'm tired, just ready to head home."

"Well then, I'll make this quick. I'd like to offer you the position of executive chef of our San Antonio location of The Starling."

I narrowed my eyes and returned my focus to him.

"Why not Kat?"

His shoulders shrugged with disinterest.

"I'm not looking for someone who can create the same dishes as everyone else fresh out of culinary school. I want someone who cares about the basics. Someone who makes the ordinary taste *extraordinary*."

"I think you can find plenty of people who can cook burgers and fries for you," I snorted, pushing a hand through my hair.

"True. But there's passion in your cooking. You're one of the few chefs I've met recently who cares as much about a burger as you would your family. There's soul in your food, and that's what I want in San Antonio."

I pushed my mouth to the side, already knowing what my answer was.

"I'm sorry, I can't accept your offer. Thank you, but I think Kat is the better choice. My life is in Seattle, and I'm not interested in relocating."

I turned to leave when he stopped me with his sharp tone.

"Then I'll offer you a position in Seattle."

I forced myself to take a long, slow breath and then blew it out gently.

"I'm sorry if I've somehow given you the impression that I'm interested in pursuing employment with you. I'm happy where I'm at but thank you so much for the compliment. Have a good evening."

I didn't wait for him to say anything else before I walked away.

The next day, it felt weird to go straight to the food truck and not to Ambrosia. Now that the competition was over, it was almost bittersweet that I didn't have a reason to go in to see Kat anymore. I'd enjoyed working alongside her in the kitchen, even if she was a flustered mess around me the majority of the time.

But now it was business as usual, so I focused on preparing everything for another busy night. Darryl had shown up at the same time as Anthony, and suddenly, it felt too cramped in the confined space of the food truck.

Today's menu consisted of a repeat of the dishes I'd served last night for the competition. Bacon avocado cheeseburgers with sweet potato fries and caramel cheesecake bars. It was simple and easy, which meant we didn't need three of us prepping.

I guided Darryl on shaping the beef into patties to make it easier once we got busy and left Anthony chopping the lettuce, onion, and tomato. There wasn't anything for me to do, so I left and went to the coffee shop down the street. I had been struggling all day after a shitty night last night, so some caffeine was much needed right now.

When I first got there, there was a short line of people, but it moved relatively quickly. I placed my order and then stepped to the side and waited. The bell dinged above the door, and I didn't have to look up to know who'd walked in. My body was automatically pulled to hers by some magnetic force that made it nearly impossible to stay away.

Kat looked down at her phone, barely paying attention as she got in line. Her curly black hair was down and shielded her face as her fingers flew across her phone. I was so deeply engrossed in watching her that I didn't hear the barista call my name until he repeated it, this time loud enough to grab her attention as well.

I swallowed hard, pushing past the lump that had taken up residence in my throat, and grabbed my coffee from him.

Kat's eyes stayed on me as she made her way up the line. I stalled for a few minutes, grabbing a sleeve for the to-go cup, even though it wasn't that hot.

I was flinging sugar packets against my finger as if I was going to add all eight of them to my coffee. It was another distraction, but it worked. Soon, Kat had placed her order and stood next to me at the counter.

"Hey," she said softly.

"Hi."

I wasn't sure where things stood between us after last night.

"Look," she sighed heavily. "I'm sorry about last night. I was out of line."

"It's fine," I assured her, taking a sip of coffee. "Let's just move forward and put it behind us."

"Okay," she nodded and tucked a stray curl behind her ear.

The barista called her name, so she turned and grabbed her coffee, then walked out with me.

"So, I have some news," she said casually, looking straight ahead of her instead of at me.

"Yeah?"

I stopped walking and gently led her to the side by her elbow.

She blew out a shaky breath, then finally lifted her eyes to mine.

"I got offered an executive chef position at The Starling in San Antonio."

I took another sip of coffee and allowed the heat from the liquid to burn my throat and force away the tightness from her words.

"Congratulations."

"Thank you."

I pulled my brows together and studied the angst on her face.

"What's wrong? Aren't you happy about it?"

"I am," she hesitated, then chewed her nail.

"But?"

She scanned the people on the street as if looking for her answer.

"But I'm scared to leave Seattle. Everything I know and love is here. My work. My friends. You."

She swallowed hard and blinked quickly to hide the tears that teased at the corners of her eyes.

I reached over and wrapped my arm around her waist, pulling her into me.

"It's a big change," I acknowledged.

"It is," she breathed and then looked up at me. "Come with me?

My heart ached at the way she begged with her eyes, desperate for me to say yes. And while I would love to follow Kat through the depths of the world, I couldn't leave my grandma.

"I'm sorry," I said softly, feeling her pull away. "I can't. Seattle is home. This is where I'm meant to be."

<u>Twenty</u>

Kat

"So, are you excited?" Jamie asked as we watched the kitchen staff bustle past us. We had just opened and were waiting for the first few orders to be done so we could check them.

"I don't know. I'm trying to be."

"How could you not be? This is like your dream come true! Okay, maybe not the moving to San Antonio part, but working for Luka Fagiolo."

"I know," I sighed. "I've been thinking about it for days since he called and offered me the job. And yes, it'll be fun and exciting to explore a new city, but I just don't feel as enthusiastic about it as I thought I would be."

It had been almost a week since the competition and Luka offered me the job. In that time, I'd kept myself busy at work and refused to stop and think about what was really bothering me.

"Are you afraid to leave Seattle?" she pressed, knowing I didn't have any family here. I was an only child, and my parents lived back east and never bothered to visit. I wasn't close with them and had only a handful of friends before I left. Since I'd moved to Seattle, I'd felt like I finally found myself and wanted to plant roots here. The people were kind. I loved my job. And most importantly, I'd found a family in the people that I worked with.

It would be hard to walk away and leave all of that behind. But then again, I'd already reached the top of where I could go with Ambrosia, so the next step should be to take the job in San Antonio. To be an executive chef at a restaurant of that magnitude would be an amazing thing to add to my resume.

"Yes and no," I blew out in a breath. I stopped to inspect the dishes that were about to go out while Jamie tended to another set. Once approved, they went on their way, and we continued our conversation.

"I don't want to leave Seattle, but I also feel like I would be missing out on the opportunity of a lifetime if I didn't follow through with this. I've already accepted the job offer and put in my notice here. I don't think it matters much at this point."

She squeezed my shoulder reassuringly.

"You'll do just fine."

I felt the warmth in her words, but that did nothing to stop that doubt that was echoing through my head.

Twenty-One

Kat

Three Weeks Later

My first week at The Starling had turned out to be a complete and total disaster. Aside from the customers who were irate that there were longer wait times because I was still trying to get into the groove of things, the staff who had no respect for the privileged girl who swooped in and stole a job many of them had their eye on, and a kitchen fire—I'd had enough.

When Alissa approached me last night and said, *you're on fire*, I thought she'd finally come around and was embracing me. I'd felt on fire for the first time while I had the kitchen running in excellent condition and with no mishaps along the way. She was the sous chef and had daggers in her eyes the moment she met me. I was under the impression that maybe she'd had a change of heart and was open to getting to know me until I felt the heat climb the length of the apron and singe the hairs on my body. I was literally on fire.

When I got home, I opened a new bottle of wine and plopped down on the couch in the small studio apartment I already hated. It was in a busy part of town, and aside from the loud street noise outside, I also had neighbors that kept me up all hours of the night. On one side, I had some college-aged frat guys who partied nonstop and then had loud sex with random women—the sound of everything floating easily through the thin walls. Then on the other side, I had a couple who did nothing but fight all the time. The constant sound of screaming and breaking things left me in a steady state of anxiety.

It was barely after eleven, and I knew Jamie would still be up, so I sent her a text message to see how things were going there. While I didn't want the full details of how great things were without me, I wanted to be supportive and see how she liked her new position as executive chef.

I'd been surprised when she told me that Clarissa had offered Miles the sous chef position and even more surprised when Jamie said he'd declined it. He insisted that he loved running Miles High Food Club, yet she said he hadn't been there much lately, leaving Darryl and Anthony to run it while he was gone.

Miles and I had texted a few times since I'd arrived in San Antonio, but it was quick and impersonal. I think we both wanted more but knew that we couldn't have it, so we stopped trying to make this thing work as a long-distance relationship. Just because we had insane chemistry didn't mean we were destined to be together. Or at least that was what I tried to tell myself every day when the pain of missing him became unbearable.

I hadn't planned to get attached to Miles. I had spent so much of my time purposely avoiding him for this very reason. I knew better than to let my guard down, but it happened anyway.

A few minutes later, I saw the dots bounce on the screen as she typed, then stopped. Then typed, then stopped. Suddenly, my phone buzzed in my hand as her name lit up the caller ID on my phone.

"Hey," I said, a little too eager to hear her voice. "You didn't have to call if you're busy."

"I'm not," she laughed. "I'm grabbing food real quick, then heading back to wrap things up."

"Must be nice," I teased.

"It is. Our new sous chef is good, but Clarissa wanted to test them on their own tonight during the rush to see how they'd do, so I got to sneak out for a bit."

Her voice changed slightly at the end, and I noticed a hint of guilt.

"I'm sure they'll do great," I said, even though I didn't know the person they'd hired to fill Jamie's spot. "So, where are you?"

I closed my eyes and pinched the bridge of my nose, regretting that I was desperate enough to ask.

"Miles High," she said quietly. "It's Greek night, and I was really craving a gyro."

I smiled though she couldn't see it, then wiped away the tear that slid down my cheek.

"Well, I won't keep you so you can enjoy your break. Call me later, okay?"

I was about to hang up the phone when she stopped me.

"Kat," her tone was sharp. "You know you can talk to me, right? Just because I'm getting food here doesn't mean I'm choosing him over you."

Before I left for San Antonio, I'd confessed everything to Jamie and cried on her couch while indulging in a carton of ice cream we shared. She knew about my heartache and that Miles and I were still trying to be friends, though we couldn't seem to get past our feelings that had developed for each other, which only made me leaving that much harder.

"I know," I hiccupped, embarrassed that we were having this conversation. "I'm just tired, and it's been a long week. I'll check in later."

"Okay. I'll talk to you soon."

I hung up the phone, tossed it beside me on the couch, and covered my face in my hands as I cried.

Twenty-Two

Miles

Two Weeks Later

"Okay, what do you need from me to get this started?" I asked, leaning forward as my grandma subtly squeezed my knee beneath the table.

"We have some paperwork we'll need to complete, but since you've already secured the funding, we can get started on this as soon as you'd like."

I grinned like an idiot, then looked at my grandma, who was beaming proudly.

I took the pen the realtor offered and started signing the stack of papers she'd set in front of me.

After Kat left, I'd found myself walking around Seattle more often than I had in the short time I'd lived there. Darryl and Anthony were pros at handling the food truck, and I was rarely needed there anymore. They knew the recipes better than me now and had even added in a few of their own.

Shortly after the competition, Clarissa offered Darryl a full-time position at Ambrosia, but he turned it down after confirming he could continue working for me. He was doing well and continued to stay with Erick, helping with stuff around the house to earn his keep. He'd even offered to pay rent, but Erick had refused his money and asked if he could help him renovate some of the outdated rooms and add on to the back of the house. It'd been a match made in heaven and allowed Darryl the flexibility to save up the money he'd made from Miles High Food Club.

During one of my many walks, I'd come across an abandoned building that was close to a homeless camp. I knew instantly that I wanted to purchase it and turn it into something that could help them.

One night, my grandma, Erick, and I sat down and discussed options. They both knew how dear to my heart it was to give back to the community, and Erick had a contact that helped me with getting a business loan to buy the building. I knew that my business model was different than most and that it was risky with what I wanted to do, but that didn't stop me.

Once we finished signing all the paperwork, I took my grandma to dinner to celebrate this new chapter in our lives.

"To new beginnings," I toasted, lifting my glass in the air as my grandma, Erick, Darryl, Anthony, and his girlfriend joined me. "Thank you all so much for embarking on this new adventure with me."

"Cheers," they replied in unison, the sound of the flutes clicking together and filling the air around us.

I blinked the tear away and took a sip of champagne.

"I still can't believe you're closing Miles High Food Club," Anthony said with a warm smile. "Now how are you going to pick up drunk women at two in the morning?"

I laughed and rolled my eyes.

"Hey, Miles High Food Club will still be there, just not as a food truck." I exhaled heavily as the words rolled off my tongue. "Plus, I could use a break from the drunk women."

Everyone laughed, lightening the mood around us.

It had been hard to announce that I was closing the food truck down this week, but it was reassuring that Darryl and

Anthony agreed to come on board when I offered them jobs a few weeks ago.

I had been able to take out enough in the loan to pay them for an entire month before the new restaurant opened, and Lord knew that I needed all the help I could get to get the place up and running on time.

It was a short deadline that I'd given myself, but people came together and volunteered to help out however they could. Erick had insisted that he would bring the guys staying with him by next week when we officially broke ground on the new Miles High Food Club. Now that everything was in place and we were ready to get started, it felt surreal and a little hard to swallow.

"What do you think?" Anthony asked, pulling me away from my thoughts.

"I'm sorry," I apologized with a shake of my head. "What were you saying?"

"I said that Clarissa stopped by the truck earlier and asked if you wanted her to put you in contact with some of the vendors she used. Jamie also offered to come by and help set up the kitchen once you're ready."

"Oh, yeah, that sounds great. Thanks."

Whenever I thought about Clarissa or Jamie, my mind immediately went to Kat. It'd been five weeks since she left for San Antonio, and I hated that we left things the way we did between us. It wasn't like we were angry with each other or fighting, but pretending there wasn't something there when there was, was just as hard.

Jamie had mentioned a few times that Kat was doing great and loving her new job, so I tried to be happy for her, but I wasn't. I missed her more than I could have ever imagined. But her happiness was all I'd ever wanted, so I sucked up my feelings and tucked them to the side with the grief I'd never dealt with after losing my dad and moved on.

Twenty-Three

Kat

Two Weeks Later

"I need seven lobster tails, three shrimp scampi, and two sirloins medium," I called out, hating how aggressive my voice sounded. Instead of the *yes, Chef,* I was used to hearing at Ambrosia, I got a lot of mumbled jargon and what I could swear was a handful of curse words.

I added the ticket to the rack and tried to steady my breathing. It was a Friday night, and the reservation list was long enough to keep us here until two in the morning by the time we caught up on the orders rushing in. *I missed Ambrosia. I missed my old coworkers. I missed Miles.*

My palms were sweating as I focused on everything happening around me. Alissa was off to the side, bossing people around without discussing anything with me first, which showed who she thought was in charge of this kitchen. I refused to let it bother me and tried to take the reins again.

"Where are the orders ready to go out?" I yelled out, raising my brows to the line of chefs in the back who were talking instead of focusing on cooking the food in front of them. "We don't have time for chit-chat; let's go!"

I turned to check the expo station when I noticed Luka lingering in the corner, watching everything with a frown and his lips pinched between his fingers.

Before I could obsess over what he was doing there and whether he was disappointed in my leadership, a server came flying through the kitchen doors with a tray of food and a scowl.

"What this time?" I asked, grabbing the ticket from her hand and examining the dishes.

"They'd like to know if the chef has cooked here before," she replied snarkily as Luka joined us. "The steak is overcooked, the salad was supposed to be plain, lobster tail not cooked thoroughly, and the toddler decided that they don't like chicken anymore."

I pinched the bridge of my nose and closed my eyes.

Luka took the ticket from me and then barked orders at the kitchen staff, getting a collective *yes, Chef* from everyone in the room except me.

"May I see you in my office?" he asked quietly.

I looked at Alissa, ready to ask her to take over but found a smug smile already set on her face as she turned on her heel and started giving orders again.

I followed him down the long hallway and stepped inside. He closed the door behind us, walked around the mahogany L-shaped desk, and sat down. He nodded to the empty chair across from him, so I sat down and folded my hands in my lap.

"You're not focused tonight," he commented without empathy, just stating the facts.

"No sir."

"Why's that?"

I shrugged and leaned back against the plush chair.

"They don't respect me. It's been a hostile environment since I got here. I've given it weeks—months even, and nothing has changed. I knew it would be difficult for everyone to adjust to an outsider, but it shouldn't take this long."

He nodded and steepled his fingers in front of his face.

"I will call a staff meeting and address the issue," he stated matter of factly as if that would just solve the problem.

I leaned forward, pulling all of the courage I had together.

"In all fairness, sir, I don't think that's necessary."

He arched a brow in question.

"I've dreamed of studying under you my entire life. Working at The Starling was something that I felt would somehow complete my life, but it's actually had the opposite effect." I paused and looked around his office, which was neatly decorated with framed pictures of his restaurants and newspaper clippings that showcased his success. "I'm miserable here. Nothing you say or do is going to change that. I appreciate you giving me this opportunity, but I'm hereby resigning my position effective immediately."

I stood on wobbly legs and offered him the best smile I could muster. It felt good to walk away from something that didn't bring me the happiness I wanted it to. I hadn't thought this through, but I knew there was only one thing that would give me the joy I wanted. Or better yet, one person. Miles.

"I'm sorry that we've let you down, Ms. Elliott. You are a very talented chef, and I hope you find the happiness you're looking for."

"Thank you."

I walked out of his office feeling lighter than I had since the moment I stepped off the plane and the Texas humidity sucked the life out of me. There was one place that I knew would bring back that spark of joy, and I was going to get there one way or another.

Twenty-Four

Kat

My feet tapped impatiently on the floor as I waited for the plane to land. I looked out the window and felt my heart flutter as I spotted the Space Needle, feeling the warmth spread through me that I was officially home.

While San Antonio felt like an experience I needed to try, I knew deep down that I belonged in Seattle. My heart was empty until I decided to come back. When I talked to Jamie and let her know I was coming back, she rushed to offer me the guest bedroom at their house until I could find something. My forever home.

Most of my stuff was still in storage because I didn't have time to do anything with it when I left for San Antonio. I was thankful that I wouldn't have to start over with everything since a new job and house were enough right now.

Part of me was anxious to get off of the plane and go find Miles, but I didn't know what I would even say to him. Almost two months had passed since I'd been gone, and we hadn't spoken much in that time. What started out as daily texts to check in with each other turned into a few times a week and then continually declined after that.

A woman's voice came over the speakers and gave instructions as we approached the runway. I listened to what she said, but the words went in one ear and out the other. When we finally landed, and I was able to get off of the plane, I smiled when I saw Jamie and her husband waiting for me at baggage claim.

She opened her arms, pulling me into a tight hug as her husband took my carry-on luggage and stepped to the side to give us space.

"I'm so happy you're back," she cried. "I missed you so much."

"I missed you too," I said, wiping the tears from my face.

"Okay, let's get you situated, and then we can go to dinner."

"Sounds great, I'm starving."

The drive to Jamie's house was quick, with little traffic. I left my suitcases in the guest room, not bothering to unpack them yet. I didn't have a job which meant I had plenty of time to tackle that stuff in the next couple of days while job hunting.

I freshened up my makeup and pulled my hair into a ponytail, not sure where they wanted to go for dinner. There were so many places that I'd missed while in San Antonio, so I wasn't picky. Though part of me hoped she would pick Ambrosia so I could have an excuse to pass by Mile's food truck.

As if reading my mind, Craig, Jamie's husband, turned the corner and parked in the lot behind Ambrosia.

"I hope this is okay," Jamie said, turning to look at me from the passenger seat as she undid her seatbelt. "Everyone is excited to see you."

"It's perfect."

I got out and walked around the front with them, trying to keep my nerves calm as we approached the line of food trucks. When we got closer to Ambrosia, my heart dropped when I noticed that Miles High Food Club wasn't there. Nothing was there. It was just an empty spot like the one in my heart.

Jamie read the frown on my face and smiled sadly.

"He closed last week."

"For good?"

She nodded and stepped inside as Craig held the door to Ambrosia open for me. Why hadn't he told me? I knew that we'd drifted apart during the time I was gone, but this was huge, and I felt disappointed that he hadn't bothered to let me know what was going on.

As much as I wanted to ask more questions about what happened with Miles, I was immediately overwhelmed by my *family* coming to welcome me home.

Clarissa had prepared a special menu just for us, and I was treated like royalty as everyone fought over who got to take care of our table. I tried to ignore the sadness as I enjoyed being home. This was where I belonged.

Once we were done, I went outside for a breath of fresh air while Jamie stayed behind to answer some questions Clarissa had about the new menu she'd been working on. That was the thing about being an executive chef; you never really had a day off.

I looked up at the sky, enjoying the cool air as it rushed over me and started to blow all of the tension and worry away.

Twenty-Five
Miles

I was working in the back when I heard the front door open, and a woman called out. I put the hammer down, wiped my hands on my jeans, and headed up front. It wasn't unusual to have people stopping by due to the ads we had posted for different jobs we needed to be filled, but I definitely wasn't expecting to see the person standing in the empty room before me.

Her back was turned away from me as she scanned the room, but I immediately recognized the hourglass figure and curves of her hips that I had gripped and held onto the night we fucked at Ambrosia. Her hair was longer, the dark curls touching the middle of her back, and her skin slightly tanned from the Texas skies.

"Can I help you?" I asked, catching her off guard as she spun around and looked startled to see me.

She blinked several times as if she couldn't believe her eyes.

"What are you doing here?" she asked, slowly stepping toward me while avoiding the debris that still needed to be swept up.

"I work here." I spread my feet apart and folded my arms over my chest, not missing the way her eyes traveled over my biceps as my t-shirt pulled snugly against me. "What are you doing here?"

She frowned and looked around as if trying to find something.

"I came to apply for a job. My friend gave me this address and said they were looking for an executive chef. I'm not sure I'm in the right place; I couldn't find a sign outside."

I felt the corners of my lips tug up into a smile.

"You're in the right place," I assured her.

She studied me nervously.

"So, why are you looking for a job?" I asked, desperate to hear her say that she was back for good.

"Things didn't work out the way I wanted them to in San Antonio."

We stepped closer to each other, the pull between us too strong to ignore.

"You didn't like it out there?"

She shook her head and wiped away a tear.

"It was horrible. They were mean to me. I didn't fit in," she shuddered a breath. "And there was something really big that I was missing there."

"What's that?" I asked, gently brushing her tears away with my thumb.

"You."

She closed her eyes and cried harder as I pulled her into my chest and held her.

"I've missed you so much," she sobbed.

"I've missed you too. More than you could ever know."

She clung to me for a few minutes before pulling away and wiping her face.

"How could you not tell me that you closed the food truck?" she blurted out with a frown.

I chuckled and then reached for her hand.

"Because I wanted to surprise you with this when it's ready."

She took my hand and allowed me to walk her through the empty space.

"I decided to close it down because I needed the funds from selling it to get this place up and going."

"What is it?"

"It's Miles High Food Club on steroids," I laughed and squeezed her hand.

"I can see that, this place is massive!"

"It's been abandoned for a few years, but when I saw it, I knew this was what I wanted. What I needed. Even though the food truck will officially be shut down, this will take its place. Same food, same culture, just a bigger space to serve more people. Those who need some help but might not be able to ask for it. People like my dad before he died."

Her eyes filled with tears again.

"Shh, it's okay," I whispered and hugged her again. "I wasn't able to save him, but I'll continue to honor him every day by helping those like him. My dad lived on the streets for years and refused to get help. I found Darryl in need of help, and when he accepted it, I felt this energy rush through me and knew that this was what I was called to do in life."

"That's beautiful. I'm so proud of you."

"You're beautiful." I pulled her closer and kissed her lips, missing the way my body felt next to hers.

"So, are you still looking for an executive chef?" she asked when we finally came up for air.

I laughed, knowing that Jamie had been the one to tell her

that I was looking for one. Miles High wasn't really the kind of place that needed an executive chef, just a few people who knew how to cook without catching the place on fire.

"Do you know someone who's interested?" I arched an eyebrow.

"Maybe. But it depends on the benefits package."

I felt her hand slip down and grab my cock through my jeans.

"Oh, trust me, the package is quite impressive."

She giggled as I tickled her sides.

Twenty-Six

Kat

One Week Later

"Can you hand me that paint roller?" I asked, looking over my shoulder to find Miles watching me bend over the pan filled with teal-colored paint.

My shorts pulled tight against my ass and rode high enough to allow the bottom cheeks to peek through.

"I've got something we can roll," he replied gruffly, grabbing my hips and thrusting his cock against my ass without handing me the roller.

"Miles," I laughed. "The grand opening is in two days, and we're not going to be ready if we don't finish up."

"I can't focus when you're bending over and showing me what I would rather be doing instead."

"We just had sex this morning. And last night. And yesterday afternoon. All we do is have sex," I joked, allowing my head to rest against his chest as he palmed my breasts.

"See, it's not good to break our streak. I say it's sex break time, then we'll get back to work."

I turned around and planted my hands on my hips.

He wiggled his brows playfully, grabbed me by the waist, and carried me down the hall. I wrapped my legs around his waist and laughed as he rushed to our new office.

It was weird to call it *our* office, but he insisted that was what it was.

After brainstorming different ideas, we'd decided to change up the original plan for Miles High and would focus on keeping it a comfortable place to eat without the expensive price tags but a wide range of foods. Miles offered me the executive chef position, and together, we worked on creating a handful of menus for the first week we were open. We wanted to draw in as many people as possible while also focusing on those who needed it the most.

He sat me down on the edge of his desk and kissed me while holding the sides of my face.

I hadn't realized just how much I'd missed being touched until I was with Miles. I'd been engaged years ago, but it was a loveless relationship that I didn't see until he drained my bank account of twenty grand and skipped town. Miles and I had discussed my past plenty of times while I'd been staying with him over the past week, but now I only wanted to focus on my future.

"The rest of the team will be here soon," I whispered as he kissed down my shoulder and lifted the bottom of my tank top.

"They know what to do," he muttered.

"What if they come back here looking for you and catch us?"

"Then try not to fake it and give them a good show."

"Miles!" I playfully shoved at his chest as he lowered his lips to the lace of my bra and pulled it down with his teeth. "At least lock the door."

"So bossy." He pinched my nipple playfully, then rushed over and locked the door.

He stalked toward me with a hungry look in his eyes, and I knew exactly what I wanted.

I got up from the desk, pulled my shirt over my head, then

tossed it to the floor. With his eyes still locked on me, I reached behind and unhooked my bra.

He licked his lips and reached for me, but I shook my head and escaped. Standing completely topless in front of him, I sank to my knees and worked quickly to pull his jeans and boxers down.

I could feel the heat pooling between my legs as his cock greeted me. He wasn't just long but thick, and his Prince Albert piercing turned me on every time I saw it.

My eyes closed as I leaned in and licked the tip, teasingly running my tongue in circles. He hissed and wrapped his hand in my hair, holding my head in place while I wrapped my lips around him and took him into my mouth.

We didn't have much time before the others would get there, so I dove straight in and worked him through to the back of my throat while stroking the length that didn't fit in my mouth with my hand.

His thighs tensed, and I could tell he was getting close. I hallowed my cheeks, sucking even harder.

"I'm gonna come," he warned.

Knowing that was my cue, I pulled him out of my mouth, hearing the loud pop as we broke the tight suction. I leaned up, pressing my breasts together as he slipped his dick between them. He came all over my chest a few seconds later, and I loved every second of it.

"You know," he panted, trying to catch his breath. "I brought you back here to give *you* an orgasm."

"Eh," I said with a shrug as I stood up and grabbed a handful of tissues to clean myself off with while he took care of his mess. "You can make it up to me tonight."

Epilogue

Miles

1 Month Later

"I need bacon cheeseburgers and sweet potato fries all day," Kat called out, getting the kitchen started for the night. We'd been open for an entire month, but tonight was a special celebration—my grandma's birthday.

Erick had brought her in a few minutes ago, and we'd planned a menu around her favorite foods. There was a reason I'd always fallen back on making cheeseburgers and sweet potato fries, and that's because it's what I grew up on. My grandfather always made them for my grandma for special occasions or just to pick her up when she was having a bad day. It became a food of love between them, and I wanted to keep that memory and feeling alive for her.

Not only that, but we were also celebrating her ninetieth birthday, and I was determined to go all out. She wouldn't allow me to throw her a party at her house or mine, so I did the next best thing—threw her a party at Miles High.

I grabbed Kat by the waist and tilted her back for a kiss while the kitchen staff bustled around us.

"Get a room," Anthony teased as he passed by with a few orders.

It was a low-stress night for us, with most of our customers being friends and family here to celebrate my grandma. What I loved the most was that almost every night felt the same.

From the day we'd opened, I'd kept to my promise of helping the community that needed it. At the end of each night, I'd take all the food we couldn't use and make meals to be delivered to as many people as possible in the homeless camps around us.

I took time getting to know everyone and, on occasion, took Kat with me. We'd met a few people who were looking for help to get back on their feet and offered them jobs at the restaurant, helping out until Erick had room for them at his place.

Darryl lived there permanently and had struck up quite the friendship with Erick. Together, they'd expanded and renovated the house, creating more space to take in more people who needed it. With the extra mouths to feed, Darryl decided to take over as the house chef and did an outstanding job.

I helped finish the plates that were ready to go out and added an extra side of the garlic aioli sauce that my grandma loved so much.

"She's going to love it," Kat said, rubbing my back reassuringly. "Now get that tray out there before those plates get cold."

"So bossy," I teased, then lifted the tray and carried it to the dining area.

She followed me and smacked my ass when she thought no one was looking.

I set the tray down on the stand she'd grabbed and set up.

My grandma's eyes lit up, and she clapped her hands excitedly as I set her plate in front of her.

"You remembered," she whispered, tears flooding her eyes.

I bent and kissed the top of her head.

"How could I forget?"

She wiped her tears away with the backs of her hands and then looked up at me.

"He would be so proud of you."

I smiled sadly, missing my grandpa more today than usual.

"I wish Pop was here to see this."

"Me too," she sighed. "But I meant your dad. He would be proud of you and what you're doing."

The tears stung my eyes as I tried to force them away.

"I'm proud of you too," Kat whispered, pulling me into her as she hugged my sadness away.

My life wasn't perfect, but it made me feel good knowing I was doing something to help others. Not only that, I had the most incredible woman in my life, and tonight I was going to ask her to be mine forever.

****

Thank you so much for reading Kat and Mile's story! I hope you enjoyed it! Want more? I have a SUPER STEAMY bonus epilogue here:

https://dl.bookfunnel.com/qbrwjb3h7q

Looking for more heat and spice? Be sure to check out my Beaumont Creek Series! Just One Time will be sure to satisfy your needs!

https://books2read.com/u/3G52zK

Did you grab your free book yet? I have a super-steamy novella about an author who eavesdrops on her sexy neighbor for *inspiration* for writing her sex scenes. You can grab your copy here:

https://dl.bookfunnel.com/5dkljhqur4

Other Books By Samantha Baca

<u>The Haven Brook Series</u>
<u>(small town romantic suspense):</u>

'Til Death Do Us Part (Haven Brook Book 1)

https://books2read.com/u/m2RJNR

The Cradle Will Fall (Haven Brook Book 2)

https://books2read.com/u/b6O0QE

The Ties That Bind (Haven Brook Book 3)

https://books2read.com/u/mqgoz8

A Very Haven Christmas (Haven Brook Book 4- Novella)

https://books2read.com/u/mvqGjj

Three Strikes, You're Gone (Haven Brook Book 5)

https://books2read.com/u/mvqL2z

<u>The Dark Shadows Series (romantic suspense)</u>

Five Steps Ahead (Dark Shadows Book 1)

https://books2read.com/u/38Q0gO

Ten Seconds Too Late (Dark Shadows Book 2)

https://books2read.com/u/3JRgVB

Against The Clock (Dark Shadows Book 3)

https://books2read.com/u/m2YwoR

Out Of Time (Dark Shadows Book 4)

https://books2read.com/u/4DKMoP

<u>The Stone Creek Series (small town- novellas)</u>

Chocolate Covered Mistletoe (Stone Creek Book 1)

https://books2read.com/u/3LRk9N

Candy Coated Promises (Stone Creek Book 2)

https://books2read.com/u/mldP5Y

Pumpkin Spiced Possibilities (Stone Creek Book 3)

https://books2read.com/u/bojdwV

<u>Beaumont Creek Series (small town)</u>

Just One Time (Beaumont Creek Book 1)

https://books2read.com/u/3G52zK

Second Chances (Beaumont Creek Book 2)

https://books2read.com/u/4Aj6Z0

Third Time's The Charm (Beaumont Creek Book 3)

https://books2read.com/u/b5lEyG

Four-ever Single (Beaumont Creek Book 4)

Preorder link coming soon

Fifth Wheel (Beaumont Creek Book 5)

Preorder link coming soon

Whiskey Mountain Series (small town- novellas)

Something To Talk About

https://books2read.com/u/4X62ag

Something To Think About

https://books2read.com/u/3GWAan

Something To Believe In

https://books2read.com/u/3yVzgB

Something To Live For

Preorder link coming soon

Standalone Books

One Last Wish

https://books2read.com/u/mqg7D9

Finding Love In Apartment 2C (novella)

https://books2read.com/u/bze9aZ

Cocky Counsel: A Hero Club Novel

https://books2read.com/u/31Kzkn

All Is Fair In Food And War (novella)

https://books2read.com/u/bp8qjX

Holiday Books (novellas)

Snow Place To Go

https://books2read.com/u/4A560N

A Christmas Wish

https://books2read.com/u/4EKXpE

Blame It On The Mistletoe

https://books2read.com/u/bw1rqe

Holiday Hijinks

https://books2read.com/u/4DP6Ze

Acknowledgements

As always, I'd like to start by thanking all of the wonderful readers who picked up my book and decided to read it! Thank you! I hope you enjoyed the story!

To my alpha, beta, and ARC readers—you all are AMAZING and I truly appreciate each and every one of you. Thank you for taking the time to read another book and give me your feedback. I'm so thankful to have you on my team!

My dear family, thanks for the constant support! You'll never know how much it means to me!

To my editing team—you all do an incredible job and thank you for making my books that much better!

My wonderful girls—you'll never know how much you mean to me. I hope someday I make you as proud as you make me. Chase after those dreams, they can and will come true.

My loving, sweet, overworked husband—I promise, I'm working my butt off to get us to a point where you can retire early and we can chase our dream of traveling the world with our girls.

Thank you again for reading this novella! If you've enjoyed it and wouldn't mind leaving an honest review on your favorite platform, I would greatly appreciate it!

About the Author

Samantha lives in the southwest with her husband and two small children after abandoning her childhood dream of living in a cabin in Colorado when she found that she couldn't afford to live there and was deathly allergic to the woods. When she's not writing, she's usually spouting off sarcastic remarks while drinking wine out of a coffee mug to look like a functional adult while chasing down her toddlers. She enjoys spending time with her family, watching reruns of Friends, and the 24/7 flow of coffee that can be found in her veins. Be sure to follow her on social media for updates on what she's working on.

You can find her here:

Facebook: https://www.facebook.com/AuthorSamanthaBaca

Instagram: https://instagram.com/author_samantha_baca

Goodreads: http://www.goodreads.com/authorsamanthabaca

Facebook Reader Group:

https://www.facebook.com/groups/2945710968775398/

Webpage: https://authorsamanthabaca.wordpress.com

Newsletter: http://eepurl.com/g0NcSj

www.ingramcontent.com/pod-product-compliance
Lightning Source LLC
Chambersburg PA
CBHW061544310726
48972CB00008B/2601